5539

D1113848

BATTLE OF THE BANDS

MIDDLE SCHOOL MAYHEM 4

C.T. WALSH

FARCICAL PRESS

COVER CREDITS

Cover design by Books Covered
Cover photographs © Shutterstock
Cover illustrations by Maeve Norton

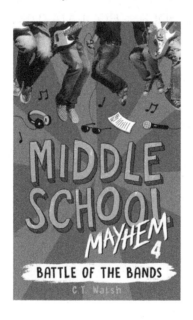

Publisher's Cataloging-in-Publication Data

provided by Five Rainbows Cataloging Services

Names: Walsh, C.T., author.

Title: Battle of the bands / C.T. Walsh.

Description: Bohemia, NY : Farcical Press, 2019. | Series: Middle school mayhem, bk 4. | Summary: Tired of being unpopular, Austin and his crew sign up for a Battle of the Bands competition. | Audience: Grades 5 & up. | Also available in ebook and audiobook formats.

Identifiers: ISBN 978-1-950826-03-2 (paperback)

Subjects: LCSH: Bildungsromans. | CYAC: Middle school students--Fiction. | Middle schools--Fiction. | Jealousy--Fiction. | Bands (Music)--Fiction. | Bullying--Fiction. | Humorous stories. | BISAC: JUVENILE FICTION / Social Themes / Adolescence & Coming of Age. | JUVENILE FICTION / School & Education. | JUVENILE FICTION / Humorous Stories. | JUVENILE FICTION / Boys & Men.

Classification: LCC PZ7.1.W35 Bat 2019 (print) | LCC PZ7.1.W35 (ebook) | DDC [Fic]--dc23.

For my Family

Thank you for all of your support

1

I'm going to let you in on a little secret. Nerds have one chance, just one, to be cool in middle school and high school. If you can't catch a football or don't look like a movie star with a butt chin like my brother, here is my advice to you: start a band. It doesn't even have to be that good of a band. You just have to be able to say that you're in one and it has to have a good name. Something cool. Something that gives you street cred. I don't know where some of these famous bands today get their names. I mean, Twenty One Pilots? Are there really twenty one pilots in the band and if so, why? What are they actually all doing? And what about Weezer? Do they all have asthma? Sounds like half the kids in my robotics club, not a band.

I had never even thought about being in a band for the first ten years of my life. I didn't even know I liked singing or was even good at it until my first year in middle school when I tried out for the holiday musical, Santukkah! But that's a story for another time. You may have even heard it already. But back to the band. It all started after I had made it through sixth grade at Cherry Avenue Middle School and we were off for a glorious summer vacation. As far as I was concerned, there were two good things about middle school: weekends and summer vacations. I was pumped to have ten weeks of summer ahead of me.

I mainly spent my summers at Camp Cherriwacka, a day camp near my house that I liked, for the most part. But camp wasn't a total escape from the chaos that was middle school. A lot of the kids from Cherry Avenue went to camp with us. So did other middle schoolers from other districts. So, the usual rules and social hierarchy still applied, but everyone was a little more laid back and spread out.

On my day of camp, the bus pulled up to Camp Cherriwacka's entrance and screeched to a stop. Ben and I hopped out first with our friends, Sammie, Luke Hill, and Just Charles behind us. My brother (the one with the giant butt chin and so very annoying) and his friend, Jayden, sat in the back with the cool kids. We were in the same grade, but he was almost a year older than me and a lot better at most stuff than I was. That's not why I didn't like him or his butt chin, but I won't get into that now.

As we walked through the wooded pathway heading toward the common area, there was a boy sitting under a tree just off the path. He paid us no attention as he played an acoustic guitar, singing to himself. He had dirty blonde hair that waved down to his shoulders.

"Man, I wish I was that cool and could do that," I said.

"Who is that guy?" Ben asked.

"I don't know. This camp pulls in from a few different schools. He wasn't here last year."

"I thought your dad taught you how to play the guitar a few years ago?" Sammie asked. We had been friends since she moved next door to me when we were three.

"He did, but I never got that good and it's been a while

since I've even picked one up," I said, as we continued walking.

A man in cargo shorts, a Hawaiian shirt, and an over-sized safari hat stood next to the pool entrance with a smile on his face even bigger than his hat. "Good morning!" he bellowed. Well, as much as you can bellow with a high-pitched, nasally voice. "You can put your bags near the cabana and gather 'round the pool."

We walked into the pool area. My sister, Leighton, was setting up a breakfast buffet on the other side of the pool. She looked over and waved to me. I waved back and then threw my stuff on the ground. It was Leighton's first year as a camp counselor at Camp Cherriwacka. There were a few other counselors around as well. Some I knew from previous years. Others were new, like Leighton.

I felt a tap on my shoulder, so I turned around. It was Sophie, my girlfriend. I was so happy to see her. I greeted her with my customary, "Hey!"

"Hey," she said back. Our relationship was so deep, we didn't really need to say much to each other. Or at least that's what I kept telling myself.

"I'm so glad Sammie talked you into coming to camp," I said.

"Me, too. I heard it's really fun."

As the kids gathered around the pool, the man from the entrance stepped forward, still with the same smile as before. I wondered if it somehow was stuck on his face. He just watched everyone as they went about their business. Nobody was that smiley all the time. I looked around at the other kids. I saw a few kids I knew from last year, a few others from school, and the guitar kid from before.

If I had a smile on my face at that time, it was most definitely gone by the time I finished scanning the group of kids. My stomach dropped as my arch nemesis, Randy Warblemacher, entered in slow motion.

Randy was a cool kid, at least that's what most of the idiots at school thought. I was not at all a fan. He was a liar, a cheater, and a bully. But man, did he have glorious hair and a fabulous singing voice. He handed his bag to the smiling man and shook out his hair like he was in a shampoo commercial. His golden lochs bounced around like homecoming cheerleaders. Sammie and a few of the other girls giggled. Ditzy Dayna nearly fell over. Randy grabbed his bag back and dropped it off next to the rest of them.

The smiling man stepped forward and said, "Good morning, campers! My name is Kevin Quackenbush. I am the new camp director. We're going to have a fabulous summer. Who's ready to have some fun?" he yelled.

We were middle schoolers, so instead of answering, we all just looked around to see who would be stupid enough to say anything. You make that mistake once. Mine was when the science fair was announced. I make no apologies. I like science.

Kevin's smile persisted. "Looks like we have a very animated group this year! You're going to meet your counselors real quick, then grab a bite to eat at the breakfast buffet, and then we have a special treat to start the summer off right. Who's with me?" he screamed, excitedly.

Silence. "Excellent! You all have your group numbers. We'll line the counselors up in order. Go get to it, campers!"

I turned to Sophie and said, "See you later." I watched her as she walked toward Leighton with Sammie. My sister was going to be my girlfriend's camp counselor. Leighton and I got along better than Derek and I did, but I still wasn't sure this whole thing was a good idea. I was just glad Derek and Randy were in a different group.

I stopped in front of camp counselor number four, Brody Foster. Ben, Luke, Just Charles, the guitar kid, and a few others all stood in silence.

Brody stood a foot taller than most of us. I guessed that he was a few years into high school. He brushed the hair out of his eyes and stepped forward. I was excited to hear about all the cool things we would be doing this summer. Camp Cherriwacka always had awesome new stuff to do.

Brody cleared his throat and said, "This is going to be a great summer experience for you. Just pretend I'm not here. I mean, I'll make sure none of you die or anything like that, if I can, but I'll mainly be on my phone or trying to get that cute new counselor to go out with me."

Ben nudged me and said, "Dude, I think he's talking about your sister."

Brody continued, "So, we're the dork group. They put all the jocks together in one group and you guys together. You know, it's like the zoo. They don't want to mix predator and prey. Death is bad for business." He shrugged. "I guess that's it. Enjoy the breakfast and the music. We'll meet back here after. Maybe." Brody walked away.

I looked at my friends. "Geez, that's harsh."

The guitar kid stepped toward us, shaking his head. "Dorks? You think I would be in the dorks' group? We're the lovers, not the fighters."

Another boy followed. He had dark hair that was a tad too long for his glasses, and arms and legs that were too long for the rest of him. He was like a four-limbed spider.

"Yeah, we're lovers." Just Charles said, not entirely confident about it.

I put out my hand to shake the new kid's hand. "I'm Austin. This is Ben, Just Charles, and Luke."

He shook my hand. "You got a girl, Aus?"

"Yep. Sophie. She's here at camp. How 'bout you?"

"Nah, man. Not lookin' to settle down in the summer time, you know what I mean?"

I just nodded, but I had no idea what he was talking about. I was just thankful that any girl liked me, especially Sophie. You don't break up with a girl like Sophie because it's summer time. Amanda Gluskin? Maybe. If you were dumb enough to date her in the first place.

"Why aren't you with the cool kids?" Ben asked.

"Here's a secret for you. You can be cool without being an athlete," the still unnamed guitar kid said.

"You can?" Luke asked.

"Absolutely. I'm Sly, by the way. This is Teddy."

"That's a cool name," I said. "What's your last name?"

"Don't need one," Sly said, simply.

"Why not?" Just Charles asked.

"Because my name is Sly. That's all you need to know. How many other kids are named Sly that you know?"

"None," Just Charles said, shrugging.

"So why do I need a last name?" Sly looked over at the breakfast buffet. "Breakfast is served. Catch you guys later, yo." Sly walked over toward the buffet with Teddy on his heels.

"He never told us the secret," Just Charles whispered, disappointed.

"Man, that dude is cool," I said.

"Yeah. People with one name are so cool," Ben said.

Luke added. "And he plays the guitar."

I walked back over to the buffet and grabbed a plate next to Sophie. She smiled at me and said, "I love your sister," Sophie said, enthusiastically. "She's awesome. How's your counselor?"

"Umm, not as good as yours."

"Awww, that's so sweet. I didn't know you felt that way about your sister," Sophie said, smiling.

It wasn't what I meant. I wasn't giving my sister a compliment. It was more about Brody stinking up the place, but I wasn't going to correct her. She called me sweet.

And then seemingly out of nowhere, Kevin Quackenbush called out, "I give you Goat Turd!"

Most of the campers cheered. Goat turd? Why the heck did the camp director want to give us goat poop? I looked over at Kevin and he was pointing at a rock band of five musicians that promptly started playing.

Most of the girls in camp rushed toward the mini stage and started shrieking like wackos.

"Oh, my God! That's Cameron Quinn!" Sammie said, nearly knocking me over. "He's so cool!"

"Who the heck is that?" I asked.

"He's the lead singer of Goat Turd," Sophie said, like I was supposed to know that.

I was a little jealous, but Sophie wasn't nearly as crazy as the rest of them, so I just tried to focus on the performance. The girls hung on every word he sang. I must admit, he was pretty awesome. He sang like a pro as he danced across the stage. Just being able to do one of them was impressive, but together, he was a star. Even a bunch of the dudes crowded around the stage and started jumping up and down as Goat Turd rocked out.

Cameron Quinn stood next to the electric guitarist in the group near the center of the small stage. He put the mic to his mouth and yelled, "Are you ready?"

I wasn't sure what he was talking about, but the crowd seemed to. They all screamed. Cameron ran straight toward the edge of the stage and jumped off it. He soared through the air and twisted, landing on his back in the outstretched hands of the mini-mob in front of him. The kids in the crowd held Cameron over their heads, passing him through the crowd.

A girl yelled, "Oh, my God! I touched him!"

When Cameron made it to the end of the crowd, he fell gracefully to his feet, landing next to a girl by the breakfast buffet. She stared into his eyes, mesmerized, holding a piece of toast inches from her open mouth. With the microphone in one hand, Cameron grabbed the girl's toast and took a bite. He handed it back to her, turned, and ran up the few steps back onto the stage.

The toast girl yelled, "O.M.G. We shared breakfast!" She looked at the girl next to her and asked, "That's like a date, right?"

"Totally...He might've even tasted your spit, so you kinda made out with him!"

Toast Girl was giddy. I just stood there staring as Goat Turd rocked the stage. I had never seen a live show of any band that good. I wasn't going to scream like a crazy wacko, but I was in awe.

AFTER THE GOAT TURD PERFORMANCE, Sophie, Sammie, and I stood facing Ben and Just Charles, the pool behind them, munching on bagels and muffins.

Sly walked over. "What's up, guys? And girls?"

Luke looked over at a crowd of girls. "Who is that with Annie Hesselbeck?"

We all looked over. I remembered Annie Hesselbeck from last year. All I really knew about her was that she was tall and always wore her strawberry hair in a ponytail. And always too tight so that she seemed confused or perhaps squinting to see what was going on in the distance. There was a girl next to her who looked like a model. The giant fan blew her blond hair back like she was on a photo shoot.

"That's Regan Storm. She's from Bear Creek. She's unlikable," Sophie said, distastefully.

"I don't think her parents even like her," Sammie said. She looked at me. "I think your sister is going to get fired for punching her in the face before the end of the summer."

Luke apparently didn't hear any of that, still mesmerized by Regan Storm. "We're lovers, right?" he said to Ben, Just Charles, and Sly.

"Yep," Sly said. "You learn fast."

"What are you talking about?" Ben asked. Apparently, Ben didn't learn as fast.

Luke said, "You heard what Sly said, 'We're lovers, not fighters.' Let's show those jocks that they've got some competition." Luke nodded in the direction of Derek, Randy, and Jayden.

"Here they come," Just Charles said, nervously.

I looked over at Ben and I could see his body start to stiffen. His muscles always froze when he got nervous. It typically ends in disaster. Hopeful that this time will be different? You shouldn't be. Like, not at all.

"What's up?" Luke said to the approaching girls.

"Hi," Regan said with a smile. Annie followed her quietly. And seemingly confused.

None of the 'lovers' in the group knew what to say. Regan walked in between the two sides of our group and stood in front of Ben. "What's up with this one? He's kinda cute."

Ben just stared at her. He usually only maintained control of his ears and his mouth. Unfortunately, he usually was able to speak, but with about half his normal brain power. This time, I wasn't sure if he still had control of his ears.

"The shy type. I like that," Regan said, stepping closer toward him. "Have you ever kissed a girl?"

We all just watched like it was the bottom of the ninth in game seven of the World Series. The home team was down by three with the bases loaded and the injured superstar was called upon to win the game with a grand slam. I know I'm a nerd, but my brother plays baseball. Anyway, none of us knew what to do. Luke's mouth was wide open. Just Charles was so nervous about Ben, he was sweating. Was she going to kiss him? Was he going to make a fool of himself? The answer is yes to one of those questions.

And then Ben spoke. "Well, my mom. And grandma. She kind of has a mustache so I have to say I don't enjoy those kisses."

I had a really bad feeling about it all, but I didn't know what to do.

Regan stepped closer to him. "Do you want to kiss me?"

"In front of everyone?" Ben asked. He looked at me. I shrugged. I know, I was a great help.

"This is going to be an amazing summer," Regan said, putting both hands on his shoulders.

"Okay." Ben puckered his lips.

Regan said, "Hashtag, are you serious, nerd?" She threw her head back and cackled. She pushed Ben with both hands and laughed as Ben teetered over like a giant statue, and fell into the pool, fully clothed, in front of the whole camp.

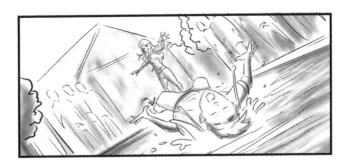

2

I rushed forward, stopping at the end of the pool. I yelled at Regan, "What's wrong with you?" Apparently, there was a lot.

Regan stepped behind me and said, "Hashtag, dork," and pushed me.

I fought it with everything I had, but she hit me like a freight train. I tumbled into the water with such force and surprise that I couldn't even take a breath. My life flashed before my eyes. Would I have enough air to ensure my survival? The answer was yes. I stood up in the shallow end to Regan and Annie laughing as they walked away.

I yelled at Regan, "I hate people who talk in hashtags!"

Ben wiped his eyes and yelled, "Me, too!"

She looked back and said, "Hashtag, don't care."

But it wasn't over. Not by a long shot. My eyes bulged as Kevin Quackenbush knocked Sophie and Luke out of the way, tossed his safari hat to the side, and yelled, "I've got you!"

Kevin disappeared under the water and stood up with

Ben in his arms. He rushed to the side of the pool and dumped him on the concrete.

"Ouch!" Ben yelled.

"I don't think he's breathing!" Kevin yelled, as he hopped up onto the concrete, one hand grabbing Ben's chin and the other pinching his nose closed.

"I'm breathing," Ben said, as if someone was pinching his nose, which was actually the case. He struggled as Kevin continued attempting to revive his already alive self.

"Hold still!"

I hopped out of the water, but I didn't really know what to do after that. I remembered when Amanda Gluskin got me in the Camel Clutch at the science fair. Without thinking, I hopped onto Quackenbush's back. As he dove in again for the mouth to mouth part of the resuscitation equation, Ben's fear scale was at its limits, which was basically Dementor's Kiss level, if you've ever read Harry Potter. The only thing I could do was put my hands under Kevin's chin and pull back, expertly executing the WWE's most devastating and embarrassing move, the Camel Clutch. "He's breathing," I yelled as I pulled.

"Snurfle nerf von schlufenterf!" Kevin said. If you speak Camel Clutch, let me know what he said, because I had no idea.

I let go, stood up, and wiped the water from my face. I gave Sophie and Just Charles the thumbs up. "It's gonna be a great summer!"

Had I still been in school, Principal Buthaire finally would've had his excuse to get me expelled. I didn't have any experience with Kevin as a camp director and I had never actually witnessed anyone getting put in the Camel Clutch at Camp Cherriwacka.

Kevin stood up and put his safari hat back on. "What the holy heck were you doing back there, camper?"

I scratched my head. "I, umm, thought you were choking. We learned the Heimlich in school."

Kevin nodded. I wasn't sure if he was still red from the Camel Clutch or fuming mad. He stepped forward, his previous perma-smile nowhere to be seen. "Way to think on your feet. You might just find yourself on the lifeguard chair down at the lake someday. With a little extra training." Kevin smiled and patted me on the back.

Kevin turned, his smile disappearing. "Regan," he called, nervously.

Regan turned, but didn't move toward us.

Kevin walked over to her and took a deep breath. "You can't push campers into the pool," he said, firmly.

Regan looked at Annie. They both rolled their eyes and then Regan said to Kevin, "Do you really think anyone cares about what you think?"

"I think your parents care what I think."

"My parents only care about how much it costs to send me here. Which is a lot of money that goes to pay your salary, Mr. Quackenbush." She paused for a moment. "I think I'm gonna call you Kev from now on."

Kevin looked down at his shoes and said, "Please be more careful around the pool."

"No problem!" Regan said.

Annie laughed as the two of them walked off together.

We had made quite the scene. The entire camp was looking at us. Of course, Randy had to say his piece.

"Ben finally got kissed! Nice work, Gordo!"

Hashtag, idiot. Sorry, couldn't help myself.

Randy continued, "Hey, Davenfart. Did you just get beat up by a girl? Again?"

"I was surprised by a girl. We didn't fight," I yelled back. I know, it was really convincing. I wasn't convinced that had it been an actual fight that I could've won, but still that wasn't the point.

"Don't listen to that idiot," Sophie said.

I shook my head as I walked over to get a towel, which was next to the food and coolers. I stared at Regan as I dried off. She walked toward me and the coolers. The crowd of people in front of her scattered like scared little mice. They were a little far from the pool to be too scared. I mean, she was still a seventh-grade girl. She wasn't the Hulk, capable of tossing kids twenty feet into the pool. Or was she? Maybe that's the only way she was able to force me into the pool despite my tree-trunk legs anchored into the concrete.

And then I saw Sly shoot me a look and a smile. He walked quickly past Regan, beating her to the soda cooler. He reached in and grabbed a soda. He turned and looked at Regan, pretending to be surprised as he shook the soda can behind his back.

"Oh, let me get that for you." Sly turned back to the cooler, grabbed another soda can and handed her the one from behind his back. "Nice move back there, by the way. The dork deserved it."

"Thanks. I saw you playing guitar before," Regan said.

"Yep. See you," Sly said.

She looked like she wanted to talk, but he didn't pay her any mind.

Regan said, "That's cool. What's your name?"

"Sly," he said, not looking back.

"My name's Regan," she called.

Sly walked by us, winked at Ben, and whispered, "Oops."

Regan popped open the can of soda. The bubbly sugar water surged from the can like a geyser, pummeling her in the face. They say that revenge is a dish best served cold. That day, revenge was a soda served cold. And shaken.

3

While the soda surprise was a minor win for Nerd Nation, it didn't even come close to getting pushed in the pool and being embarrassed in front of everyone. The cool chicks made it clear that nerds like us weren't ever going to be cool. I didn't really care what those two particular girls thought, because they were jerks, but what if all of them felt that way?

Brody was nowhere to be found, so our group sat on lounge chairs around the pool discussing the situation of our second-rate social standing. Just Charles was plugging numbers into his phone.

"My calculations suggest that we have a 0.01% chance of being cool before we graduate from college," Just Charles said, shaking his head.

"After that?" I asked.

"A solid 20% if you go the entrepreneurial route."

Ben asked, "What's the worst case?"

"Same 0.01% if you become a college professor. Turtle necks aren't cool."

I stood up and started pacing. "We need to do something about this."

Luke added, "I'm sick of being second best."

"I think we're like last, whatever number that is," I said.

Luke responded, "Not helping."

Ben didn't seem to get the hint. "Right now, the marching band flutist who wears his shoes on the wrong feet is cooler than us."

Even I didn't know it was that bad. "Timmy Griffin?" I asked. "Really?"

Just Charles nodded. "Google it, man. It's first page."

As I continued to pace, my Randy meter started going off. I looked up to see him talking to Regan past where Goat Turd was cleaning up, just outside of the pool area. Both were smiling as they talked. "A perfect match. Two horrible people."

"Huh?" Ben said.

I nodded in the direction of evil and said, "Look who's getting along."

There were a bunch of shrugs and head shakes.

Just Charles said, "We need to break the nerd cycle, but how?"

"Where the heck is Brody?" I asked.

"Probably chatting up your sister," Luke said.

"Who cares where he is? We have a big problem to solve here."

"You guys okay? Perhaps I could be of some assistance," Cameron Quinn said, approaching. He pushed his long hair back with one hand, the thumb on his other hand hanging onto the pocket of his expertly-ripped jeans.

"Nerd, girl problems," I said. "You wouldn't understand."

Cameron chuckled. "I used to be like you guys."

"What do you mean? How is that possible?" Luke asked.

"What did you do?" Ben stood up, enthralled.

"I started a band. Chicks dig Goat Turd."

"That sounds disgusting," Ben said. "Why would chicks like turds from a goat?"

"No, man. That's my band," Cameron said, laughing.

"Oh," Ben said. "Still kinda disgusting."

Cameron continued, "You gotta have something edgy. Unique."

I said, "It's certainly unique."

"I'm tellin' you man. I was a nerd a few years ago, sitting in my friend's basement, having a meeting just like this. That meeting turned into Goat Turd."

"I can't believe that. You guys are so cool," I said.

"T.J., our drummer, had more zits than friends. Vogel was so nervous around girls, he only spoke to them in sign language. Yaz wore cardigan sweaters. Every. Day. And I was the worst of us. The football team used me as a seat cushion in lunch. Sometimes they'd take me outside like I was a beach blanket or something. Three of them sat on me every day. And I'm talking the big, fat ones. Taco Tuesday was the worst."

"This is incredible!" Just Charles shrieked. He looked at Cameron and said, "Not Taco Tuesday. That's just horrible, but I'm just excited that there's still hope. I just calculated the likelihood of us being cool to be 0.01%."

"That high, man?" Cameron laughed. "I'm tellin' you, dudes. Start a band. You won't regret it. Battle of the Bands is happening at the end of the summer. Start a group and sign up! I see good things for you, dudes. I gotta run."

"Thanks," we all said, in unison.

We all watched in awe as Cameron walked back to his band mates.

I looked at my crew and said, "Let's start a band! Who's with me?"

"I'm in!" Ben yelled as he jumped up.

"Let's do this," Luke said.

Just Charles put his hand in the air and said, "Band high-five. On three." We got in a circle and readied for a team five. I wasn't good one on one. I wasn't sure about a group five. "One, two, three!"

We all threw our hands up toward Just Charles' five-fingered target. I was a little shorter than the rest of the group, standing a foot farther away, and not exactly the most coordinated of kids. Which, coupled with the excitement of no longer being a nerd, meant that my high-five was off line and turned into a face five. The palm of my hand missed the others and continued on toward Ben's face. I connected with the top of his nose. Ben's head snapped back as he screamed, back peddled, and wobbled at the end of the pool.

I rushed toward him, my arms out to grab him. Just Charles turned toward Ben as well, his foot tripping mine. I stumbled, the momentum thrusting me forward. I collided with Ben. He wrapped his arms around in a final attempt to stay on top of the concrete, but I was moving too fast. We splashed into the pool in a heap of tangled arms and legs.

As I wiped my eyes, I saw a giant blurry figure moving at warp speed. It took me a second to figure it out. "Ah, farts. Not again," I said.

Before I could do anything, Kevin Quackenbush was already airborne, soaring over a rubber ducky tube.

He cut into the water with barely a splash and surfaced with Ben in his arms. I didn't have it in me to save Ben from the Dementor's Kiss twice in one day, so I just stepped aside and let it happen, excited about our new adventure into Rock 'n Roll.

4

_____

I drank a few more iced teas at the breakfast party than my mother would approve of and had to make a pit stop. I headed over to the bathroom, which was a small pavilion on the side of the main building.

As I hurried toward the entrance, I heard voices and music echoing on the other side of the bathroom door. It sounded like they had a sweet sound system in the bathrooms. I thought it was odd, but I shrugged and pushed the door open. And then I felt a surprising warmth burst forth from inside. At first, I thought the whole place was on fire, but as I scanned the room in a panic, I realized that there was a roaring campfire in the middle of the bathroom. A group of people sat on tree logs in a circle.

They all looked at me as I let the door close behind me, but the music continued. They were singing, led by a guitarist, who had his back to me. As he strummed the acoustic guitar into the grand finale of the song, I circled around the fire. It was one of the weirdest things I had ever seen.

And then I realized who the guitarist was. It was Max Mulvihill! Max ran a private bathroom/comfort station at Cherry Avenue Middle School. I had no idea why anyone allowed him to charge people to do their business in a public school, but they did. And he ran a great business.

As Max finished the song, he looked over at me with a smile. "Aus, the boss!"

"Max, what are you doing here?" I asked, surprised.

'School's out for summer. Where do you think I'd be?" he asked, like it was totally normal to be singing around a roaring fire in the bathroom of a summer camp.

I shrugged, totally confused. "I don't know. Vacationing in the south of France?"

"That's August, dude. You wanna join us for S'mores?"

A lanky kid who looked about high school age tossed a bag of marshmallows over the fire. Max snagged it with his strumming hand and held it out for me.

"If you insist." Who can say no to S'mores?

"Have a seat. This is Amber, Jack, Chase, and T-Bone." Max pointed out each guest as he named them.

"Hey guys," I said with a wave. I looked T-Bone up and down. He seemed friendly enough, but he was a big dude who looked like he could eat a raw T-Bone steak. I sat down and put a marshmallow on the tip of a toasting stick and held it a few inches above the flame.

"Summer good?" Max asked.

I was still a little bit in shock. "Yeah, I guess. Just started a band, which I'm pretty excited about." I looked at the rest of the group and said, "You know, it's kinda the only way a nerd can break into being cool." Everyone nodded in agreement.

"I heard about your band," Max said.

"You did? It just happened like five minutes ago."

Max laughed. "I don't know how many times I have to tell you. It's my job to know."

"You never cease to amaze me, Max," I said.

"I expect you'll be the lead singer?" Max asked.

"We haven't gotten that far."

Max looked at the rest of the group and said, "Austin's quite the performer. He starred in Cherry Avenue Middle's holiday musical, Santukkah! last year. He was glorious."

"Nice work," T-Bone said in a voice so deep it didn't seem real. The others smiled, approvingly.

My face flushed red. I was embarrassed by the attention. I decided to change the subject. I looked around at the bathroom. "What's the deal here?"

"With what?"

I felt kind of stupid asking in front of all the other people, particularly T-Bone. I'm not exactly sure why. "Do I gotta pay to pee?"

Max waved me off and chuckled. "Oh, no. It's all included in the camp fees. You can poop, too," he said, as if our conversation was totally normal.

That was good, because this was the only bathroom on the premises. At school, Max had competition with the free school options. At Camp Cherriwacka, it was here or the woods. And I had no intention of doing you-know-what in a hole in the woods. Leaves don't make for good toilet paper. If you haven't tried it, just take my word for it. Maybe I'll tell you that story another time.

Anyway, I finished my S'mores and did my business, even though it was kind of weird that a girl was there. But with the stall and the music blaring, it was still pretty private. And then I said my farewells to Max, T-Bone, and the rest of the crew, and returned to my camp group.

BRODY WAS NOWHERE to be found, so we sat around under the shade of a few large oak trees. Most kids napped or messed around on their phones. My crew had better things to do. We had a band to build. We sat pretzel style in a circle. It was super rock star like.

"We need a band name. We need instruments, jobs, whatever you want to call them," I said.

Ben said, "Austin is clearly our best singer, so he's our lead singer."

"I like the sound of that. Just Charles is a beast on the piano, so you should play keyboard," I said.

"Awesome," Just Charles said.

"I like the drums," Ben said. "I mess around on my cousin's set all the time."

Luke said, "My dad plays bass."

"Darth Vader is in a band?" Just Charles laughed.

"Ha ha, very funny," Luke said. We make a lot of Luke Skywalker and Star Wars jokes with Luke because of his name. We're dorks. This should not surprise you.

I scratched my head, thinking. "I'm not a band expert,

but I think we are short a lead guitarist. Do we want to have a fifth member?"

"I think we need one," Ben said.

"It would be ridiculous not to have one," Luke said.

"Do you think Randy plays the guitar?" Just Charles asked.

I just shook my head with a smirk.

"Jimmy Trugman?" Ben offered.

"He's in Europe all summer," Luke answered.

"What about J.P.?" I asked.

"Jay?" Just Charles asked, his eyes bulging. "I'm in the band with him at school. He's brutal. When he plays the saxophone, it sounds like a seal getting run over by a dump truck."

"So that's a no?" I asked.

They all laughed. I turned around to approaching footsteps.

Brody walked up behind us. "You guys wanna do camp stuff?" I turned around to see him reading a piece of paper. "Up next, I think we have the magical world of Paper Mache."

"Hard pass!" Sly yelled while lying under a tree, his hands behind his head.

Some random kid yelled, "Paper Mache? Are you serious?"

But I wasn't really paying attention. I was still looking at Sly. He played the guitar. He would give us instant street cred.

"Are you guys thinkin' what I'm thinkin'?" I asked.

"Totally," Luke said. "Is Regan into me? I don't know the answer."

Ben smacked Luke on the arm. "Really, dude? After what she did?"

"I was kidding," Luke said, likely not kidding.

"You really know how to ruin a moment. I was talking about Sly as our guitarist," I said, shaking my head.

Luke said, "Totally."

"Done," Ben said.

"He's got my vote," Just Charles said.

Now we just had to convince Sly to join our start-up band. The original four had nothing to lose. Sly was already cool. He could've even already been a solo act. His mysteriousness made me nervous. It was going to be up to me to get him to join.

5

It was our group's turn to play lawn darts. It's not exactly the greatest game for nerds like me. Throwing sharp objects with precision is not a skill set we typically have. After Teddy took a lawn dart to the big toe and had to be rushed to the nurse's station, we didn't really do much. We really just sat around, waiting to move on to our next activity.

Sly sat under a tree, strumming on his guitar. I walked over, careful not to disturb him, and plopped down one tree over. He finished his song and looked over at me.

"What's up, man?" he asked.

I was more nervous than I thought I would be. When you get a lot of rejection, putting yourself in positions where you could get more is tough.

"I have a question for you," I said.

"Fire away," Sly said.

"Well, given recent events, we decided to start a band and well, we need a guitarist. You're pretty awesome. We were wondering if you wanted to join us?" I asked a little more higher pitched than I would've liked. I didn't want to seem too desperate.

"You guys got a good singer?"

"My mother thinks so," I said like an idiot. "I was a lead in the school musical."

"Yeah, I'll give it a shot. I think I'd like hanging out with you guys."

"Noyce," I said, attempting to turn the boring word of nice into something much more interesting. Did it work? I don't know, but sometimes you gotta shake things up.

We walked up to the rest of the crew. I smiled widely and said, "He's in, dude."

"In where?" Brody asked.

"Our new band," Sly said, smiling.

Just Charles asked, "New band high-five?"

"Probably not a great idea after the last one," I said.

"Yeah, but there are no bodies of water around," Just Charles said.

"Maybe later," I said. I looked at Sly and said, "We're the worst high-fivers ever."

"Total nerds," Luke said.

"Not anymore!" Sly said. "You're in a band now, boys. Your lives are about to change."

We were all so pumped, we had to stop ourselves from an impromptu high-five.

Brody stepped forward. "You guys starting a band?" He lit up. "As your counselor, it automatically makes me your manager. I get 10% of domestic bookings and music sales and 15% internationally."

"Really?" I asked.

"Yeah, it's in the camp paperwork your parents signed."

"Sounds questionable," Ben responded.

"Man, I can help you. Big time. I was in a band once. I

don't want you to end up like me. I can guide you. Show you the ropes. Take you to the top!"

"What do you mean, end up like you?" Just Charles asked. "You're like sixteen, still in high school."

"I think he means terrible camp counselor," Sly whispered.

~

THAT AFTERNOON, we lounged by the small lake just a short walk from the main part of camp. I thought it was kind of swampy, so I never went in, but some kids would hit the tire swing or cannonball off the end of the dock. Brody actually took some responsibility and watched the kids who were swimming, along with Mary, the lifeguard.

So, the rest of our new crew sat in a group of chairs just off the water, trying to come up with a band name. As Cameron from Goat Turd had told us so wisely, we needed a good name like his. I didn't really agree with him that poop from a goat was a good band name, but I didn't blame them for going with it, because up to that point, we hadn't had any better ideas. In fact, Monkey Poop was our leading name at that moment.

"Come on, guys. Think," I said, running my fingers through my hair, angrily.

"We're just brainstorming. You can't get mad," Just Charles said.

"You're right. Sorry. There are no wrong ideas," I said.

"Blowing Milk Bubbles," Ben offered.

"No, that's wrong. Totally wrong," I said.

Luke popped out of a chair like it was an ejector seat. His face lit up. "I got it! I got it!"

"What is it?" We all asked, eagerly.

Luke said, "Light a Fart!"

"Really?" I asked.

"What?" Luke said, defensively.

"You think chicks dig guys who light farts?" Sly asked.

"He's got a serious point," Ben said.

"Yeah, but Goat Turd?" Luke countered.

"He's got a serious point," Ben said.

"Wait a second, I got one," Just Charles said. "Bacon!"

"That's better," I said. "Definitely our best so far."

Just Charles continued making his case, "Everybody loves bacon. Come on, guys?"

"Can bacon sing?" Luke asked.

"No, but it rocks," I said.

Ben said, "What about Bacon Cheeseburger?"

"No, how about Fart Light?" Luke said, excited.

Sly shook his head. "That's the same thing as Light a Fart."

Just Charles said, "The Butt Chins. No, The Butt Heads."

"Wouldn't Principal Buthaire love it if we were The Butt Hairs?" I asked, given that most of the school called him Prince Butt Hair.

"Yeah, but then he would probably know you named him that," Ben said.

"Litter Box," Luke said.

"Outhouse?" Just Charles asked, cautiously optimistic.

Luke asked. "Is it crazy that I think we should be named, Lit Fart?"

"It's crazy that you're even asking! Enough with the fart lighting!" I yelled. "This is ridiculous."

"I got it! I got it! Portapotty!" Ben said.

"Horrible," Sly said.

"Hey, this has been real normal, but can we move onto something else and come back to this?" I asked.

"Okay," Luke said.

"What are we gonna play?" Ben asked.

"We should write a song about our haters," Luke said, pounding his fist into his palm.

"We don't have any haters," I said. "Nobody knows we even exist."

"Oh, right."

Face palm.

6

I t was a great first day at camp. We had started a band to end our nerdiness and blast ourselves off into coolness. True, we still needed a cutting-edge band name. Bacon Cheeseburger was the best one we had come up with. It did make me a little nervous about our song-writing skills.

The second day of camp was not as great. At least it didn't start off that way. Upon our arrival, I immediately found myself in the annoying radius of one Randy Warblemacher. I kept my head down as I walked with Ben, but he spotted me.

Randy walked hand in hand with Regan as he looked over at me. "Davenfart? I thought I smelled you nearby. I heard you started a lame band."

"Yep," I said, simply, and kept walking.

"So, you admit it's lame?"

"No," I said, defensively.

Randy chuckled. "Well, if it's anything like the musical, you'll be second best again."

Regan peeked around Randy and said, "Love Puddle is so amazing. They had a special practice for me last night."

"Love puddle? What the heck is that?"

"That's our band name," Randy said, defensively.

"That's the dumbest thing I've ever heard. And Luke Hill thought we should name our band Litterbox," I said.

"Love Puddle," Ben said, chuckling.

Regan said, "Litterbox. Ooh, I like that."

As we waited by the pool (not too close to the edge) for Brody to arrive to get paid to do nothing, but try to get a date with my sister, we vented.

"What does he need to start a band for? He's already a star athlete," I said, a bit whiny. Or a lot.

"That is so uncool," Luke said.

Just Charles stomped his foot. "He doesn't see me trying to dunk one of those soccer balls in the round hoop thingie!"

Luke said, "Dude, he plays basketball."

"Are you sure a band is gonna work for this guy?" Sly asked, jokingly.

"Real funny," Just Charles said, rolling his eyes.

Brody walked out of the utility room and waved. He called out as he walked toward us, "Big day, today."

"Why?" Ben asked.

"Band practice and dodge ball with Mr. Muscalini."

"Mr. Muscalini is a counselor here?" Just Charles asked, frustrated. "This day is just getting worse. First Love Puddle. Now this. If I wanted to be back in school, I would've signed up for summer school."

Personally, I wasn't sure Mr. Muscalini as a counselor was a good thing or not. I hated gym and he sometimes put me in a tough spot, but I kinda liked him. He was a good motivator.

"Can we skip dodge ball?" Ben asked.

"Nah, he's dating my mom and he got me this job. I'll get into trouble."

"Sorry to hear that," Ben said.

"Yeah, you really take the job so seriously," I said.

We followed Brody out of the pool area and down the path toward the dodge ball field, or whatever it was that it was called. As we approached, Mr. Muscalini stood with his hands on his hips, dressed in his usual too-short shorts, whistle in his mouth.

Mr. Muscalini blew the whistle three times in rapid succession and then spit it out. It bounced around his neck as he yelled, "You're late! Let's go! Move your tiny, annoying bodies. We're missing valuable dodge ball time!"

Sly looked at us, a little afraid. I had never seen him like that. I only knew him for one day, but still.

We stopped in a tight cluster about ten feet in front of Mr. Muscalini. It was a habit- the Nerd Herd. Nerds survive better in groups. The best was when you were in the middle, protected (of course, not all that well) by the nerds around you. So, when the Nerd Herd was forming, there was always some jostling and sometimes negotiating, or even begging.

Mr. Muscalini stepped forward, his ginormous quad muscles rippling like white-water rapids. "My name is Mr. Muscalini. I am in charge of physical activity here at Camp Cherriwacka. And I'm going to answer the two burning questions I know you have right off the bat. Yes, I work out. And yes, you can feel my bicep." He flexed his arm, his t-shirt stretching to its limits, threatening to tear.

I looked around at our tightly-packed group. I said, "Guys, don't worry. It's just nerds against nerds. This is easy. Nothing to the face or privates. Most of us can't even throw, let alone throw and hit someone."

A collective sigh of relief surged from their mouths. That is, until the other group arrived. Randy, my brother, Derek, Jayden, and another dozen or so hulking athletes emerged from the pathway in the trees.

"You said it was gonna be okay!" Teddy yelled at me.

"I didn't know!"

I would tell you what happened in our dodge ball match, but neither I nor any of my friends remember what happened. We all just woke up, scattered in the field, with no recollection of anything. I rolled to my side and attempted to sit up. Pain rippled through my body. I saw Mr. Muscalini bench pressing a dead tree trunk that stretched out about ten feet to each side. He tossed it off like it was nothing as we all started to stir. I looked around. The other squad was nowhere to be found.

As Nerd Nation reunited, Mr. Muscalini stood in front of us, a disappointed look on his face. "Camp's been over for about an hour. I called your mothers. We shall never speak of this again."

That was probably for the best.

THAT NIGHT, we had practice at Brody's house. We stood in his garage, hanging out and talking. The entire garage was dedicated to music. He had a full set of equipment: drums, guitars, amplifiers, microphones, a triangle and even a cowbell. I wasn't sure we were going to incorporate a triangle or a cowbell, but at least we had the option if we wanted to take advantage of it.

"What happened with your band?" Sly asked Brody.

"What was it called?" Just Charles asked. "We still need a name."

"I thought we were Lit Fart," Luke said.

"Dude!" I yelled.

"Just kidding," Luke said, laughing. "Kinda. Maybe. Not really."

Pain spread across Brody's face. "Our name was French Lisp."

"How did you come up with that?" Ben asked.

"Our lead singer had a lisp and sang in French."

"Okay, I guess that's better than Love Puddle," I said. Barely.

"Did you tour in France?" Just Charles questioned.

"No."

"Why did he sing in French?" I furrowed my brow.

"He was an exchange student. That's all he spoke. And the rest of us couldn't sing. It was awesome. None of the lyrics needed to make any sense, because none of us knew what he was saying."

Ben leaned over and whispered to me, "I think we know why they didn't succeed."

I concealed a chuckle by turning it into a fake cough.

Brody clapped his hands together and said, "Well, let's get started. There's sheet music for everyone at each station. We're going to start with 'I Shot the Sheriff' by Bob Marley."

"We're a reggae band?" Sly asked.

"No, we just play awesome music. You gotta give the people what they want."

We did a run through. It was clunky, but not overly terrible.

"Again, from the top," Brody said, officially. At least he was taking this job seriously.

We ran through the song again. It sounded a little better, but still not overly fluid.

"It's got to flow. Like a crystal-clear river," Brody said.

"That was more like chunky puke," Sly said.

I looked at Sly. He wasn't happy. "What's wrong?" I asked. He looked at Ben and then said, "Nothing."

But I knew what he was thinking. Our first gig was gonna stink.

7

We practiced every day for the next week. We had learned five songs, enough to play a short gig in front of a crowd. As long as they weren't paying, I thought we might be okay.

We gathered at Brody's garage, waiting for instructions. I was a little nervous for our first gig. I had sung in front of a lot more people during the holiday musical, but I still had the butterflies.

Plus, if we played anywhere near how we looked, it was going to be pitiful. We were all wearing something different. I wore a winter hat, pulled down to my eyes, jeans, and a t-shirt. Ben had a black mesh shirt and red headband. I don't even know where he got a mesh shirt from. Sly had ripped jeans and a jean jacket. Just Charles wore a tank top and a backwards hat. Luke wore pants that were way too tight and could barely walk, and a fake nose ring.

Brody stepped forward and said, "The guests will arrive in about fifteen minutes. We should warm up."

As we gathered our things, Ben asked me, "Who are we playing for?"

"Probably a few cats and turtles. Maybe a squirrel or two."

Ben took a deep breath. "Phew. I thought it was going to be in front of actual people."

"Ben, I was kidding," I said. Ben was not exactly Mr. Smooth under pressure, as you already know. It was my biggest concern about having him in the band. I hoped that by having him in the back, he would be far enough away from the crowd that he would be okay. I started to realize that I was wrong.

"You serious? Okay, okay," Ben said, trying to calm himself down. "You got this, Benjamin."

"Hey, man. Just pretend they are cats and turtles," I said, not sure if it would work.

"That's brilliant!" Ben said, running back to his drums.

As he passed the others, Sly said, "Ben, are you wearing a mesh shirt?"

"Yeah, isn't that what we're supposed to wear?"

"Umm, no," Sly said, eyes bulging.

After a few minutes of warm ups, the crowd started to gather. And by crowd, I meant four kids on bicycles, two old ladies with walkers, and yes, a squirrel.

"All right, this is it!" Brody said, excitedly. "Our first performance. Rock it! When you're ready."

I grabbed the microphone from the stand and looked back at Ben. He did the sign of the cross, which was weird because he was Jewish, but it wasn't for me to judge. He looked at me and nodded.

Ben smacked his drum sticks together and yelled, "One, two, three!"

The band started up and we headed into it. I didn't have a lot of room to move around, which was good, because I really had no clue how to dance, so I just held onto the microphone and the stand like my life depended on it. I tried to read the faces of the bike kids and old ladies. I couldn't tell if they were into it or not, or if the old ladies had good enough hearing to catch any of it.

About thirty seconds later, I got my answer. I closed my eyes as I hit a high note. By the time I opened my eyes, the bike kids were zipping down the street. Apparently, they had heard enough. Brody was pacing back and forth, biting his fingers and sometimes, his whole hand, seemingly as a means to keep himself from yelling at us. It was not looking good for us.

By the end of the song, the old ladies had decided to move on, but walked so slowly, I'm counting that they stuck around for two songs. The good news is that the squirrel stayed for the whole thing. We brought our grand finale to a close and looked out at the empty driveway, but for Brody. He clapped, but it wasn't the good kind. It was the slow, patronizing kind.

I think he was about to tell us how badly we did, but Mr. Muscalini drove up in a red Camaro and got out. He walked up to Brody with a huge smile on his face. Mr. Muscalini opened his hulking arms and said, "Bring it in here, son."

Mr. Muscalini engulfed Brody, who didn't reciprocate the hug. "Son? You've been dating my mom for like two months."

"Still, we've bonded like a Cy Young pitcher and an all-star catcher."

"I don't know hockey," Brody said.

Mr. Muscalini looked like his head might explode. "It's baseball! My God..." Mr. Muscalini looked up toward the heavens, but no help arrived.

"I've seen a lot of bands in my day. Mostly on the sidelines in games I was crushing it in, but still. I have a keen ear for music." Mr. Muscalini looked at me. 'By the way, how do my ears look? I've been doing electronic muscle stimulation on them, trying to bulk these bad boys up. They're the biceps of the head."

"Umm," I hesitated. "They do look bigger."

Mr. Muscalini broke into a wide smile. "Awesome! What's not as awesome? What I just heard. That sounded like an air horn that had diarrhea, like the bad kind."

Ben looked at me and said, "Is there a good kind?"

I shrugged.

Brody cut in, "Ben, you keep falling off time."

"I'm playing the notes like they're written."

"Yeah, but not on time. And it's a G not an E, Luke."

"I didn't play any E's. I don't like E's."

"And Chuck, you dropped out late."

"Don't call me, Chuck."

"Okay, how bout Charlie?"

"It's Just Charles," he said through gritted teeth.

"We're still finding our voice," I said, trying to keep the criticism from tearing down our band.

Mr. Muscalini said, "That's the understatement of the year, fellas. But on a positive note, Charles, nice tank top. Sun's out, guns out, am I right?"

"Always, sir," Just Charles said.

"And Gordo is that a mesh shirt?" Mr. Muscalini asked.

"Umm, yes sir. Nobody seems to like it," Ben said, shyly.

"I love it! Think I can borrow it?"

Ben looked at me, surprised. "It might be a little small. I'm eleven."

"Yeah, but it'll make my pecs pop. I need more mesh shirts in my life." Mr. Muscalini looked at Brody and said, "You think your mom would like me in this?"

"I, I don't know. And I don't want to know."

Sly stepped forward, looked around at all of us and said, "I think we gotta get a little more coordinated with our gear. We look like we went shopping at the Rock 'n Roll thrift shop."

Brody's face lit up. He looked at me and said, "Do you think you can get Leighton to help us there?"

"I'll try," I said. I wasn't confident, but it was a possibility.

"All right. Pack it up. Practice tomorrow. We can build from here. French Lisp was actually worse our first day than you guys were today." Brody said.

"Nice speech, son," Mr. Muscalini said. "If you ever need any pointers, I'm a master motivator."

Brody smiled and said, "Thanks."

As we packed up our stuff, Sly called out, "Hey, Ben? What are those?" he asked, pointing at the drums.

Ben looked confused. "Drums?"

"Oh, I wasn't sure because they sounded like garbage."

"Oh," Ben's face dropped.

"Just kidding, man," Sly said. He wasn't.

I didn't know what to do. Sly turned around and started packing up his guitar. Luke, Just Charles, and I stared at each other.

Ben walked past Sly without saying anything and then me, out of the garage. He nudged my shoulder as he walked by. I followed him.

"Oww. What'd you hit me for?" I asked, following him.

"Why didn't you defend me?" Ben asked, confused.

"I'm sorry. I just didn't know what to say."

"Tell him he's wrong."

"It was definitely a mean thing to say, but-"

"But what?"

"You struggle doing stuff in front of people. You get nervous and it affects you. Remember 5th grade graduation when you wouldn't stop hugging Mrs. Gerkins because you froze when you realized everyone was watching you? Mr. Chandler had to peel you off her. Or the school play? Santukkah! Or our science fair presentation?"

Ben's face morphed a deep red and he stormed off, nearly stomping on the only fan we had, the squirrel.

8

One morning before camp got into full swing, a bunch of us stood in the common area, waiting for, you guessed it, our counselors. Ben was still a little miffed at me, so I let him have his space. I talked with Sammie and Sophie.

Sammie was telling us about her birthday party plans.

"I need some cool music. A DJ or something," Sammie said.

"What about DJ Fight Club?" Sophie asked.

"That's a real name?" I asked.

"Yeah, she's awesome."

"Okay," I said, "How about a band?" I asked. "I kinda know one."

"Yeah, you guys should play for me," Sammie said.

"Totally," I said, excited at the prospect of getting our first real gig.

Before we confirmed any details, Brody, Teddy, and Luke walked over toward me.

Luke said, "We gotta talk. Sorry, ladies. Band business."

He said it like we were actually a real band that accomplished stuff.

"I'll see you later," I said to both of them, and walked over to the crew.

"Bad news," Luke said.

"What?" I asked.

"Love Puddle," Brody said.

"They just joined Battle of the Bands," Luke said.

Ugh.

Randy Warblemacher, always raining on my parade. We were on the verge of our first real gig, the launching pad to our international superstardom and he had to ruin it again. I was sick to my stomach. Our unnamed band was going to mop up his stupid puddle of love.

LATER THAT NIGHT, I decided to call Sammie to see how serious she was about having our no-named band play at her party. No answer. I texted her. She didn't respond.

When I saw her on the camp bus the next morning, I said to her, "Busy last night?"

"Yeah. Sorry I didn't get back to you. Busy with party planning. You know."

"No problem. Just wanted to see if you were serious about having our band play at your party."

Sammie's face dropped. "Oh, I'm sorry. I don't think it's going to work out. My parents got somebody already."

"Okay," I said, pretending to be okay. I wasn't happy about it, but I wasn't sure why we couldn't play, too. It's not like we were going to ask to get paid. Maybe it was because we were so bad, we didn't offer to pay her.

9

S ammie's party started at 3:00 on Saturday. Since it was so close to my house and I had nothing better to do than dodge Derek's insults and pranks, I headed over to the party early. Sophie and Ditzy Dayna would probably be there as well, helping to set up and probably doing hair and nail stuff. If that was the case, I hoped the pretzels and chips would be out. I would hang out with the two of them.

I walked into the Sammie's backyard and shut the gate. I followed a stone path around the side of the house that opened up to the bulk of the backyard. An in-ground pool was set just off a small deck. There was a barbecue and a bunch of tables and chairs with balloons. Sophie waved from the other side of the sliding glass door and came out to see me.

"Hey," I said. It was our customary greeting.

"Hey, I gotta tell you some-"

Sammie came out of the house and ran over to me. "Austin!"

"Happy birthday!" I said, and gave her a hug. I didn't

want her to feel bad about the whole band thing, so I decided to just get past it. "So, what DJ did your parents get?" I asked as cheerfully as I could, holding no resentment whatsoever.

Sammie looked down at the ground. "Oh actually, they got me a band."

I gulped. I tried to control the frustration bubbling up inside me. Or did I have to fart? I wasn't sure. No, I was getting angry. I was sure of it.

Sammie looked at Sophie and then back at me. She said, "Don't be mad."

"Okay..."

"You're gonna be mad."

I looked at Sophie. She didn't look happy, either.

Sammie continued, "My birthday present was Love Puddle."

"What?" I yelled. I took a deep breath and whispered angrily, "How could you...I can't believe you would do that to me."

And then I felt a spritz of water on the back of my head. I turned around. I didn't see anything. "What the-" I wiped the back of my head dry and looked at Sophie, who shrugged.

Sammie looked at me with puppy dog eyes. "Please don't be mad. You're one of my best friends. I just really like him. It's my birthday."

I was mad, but it was her birthday, so I pretended it wasn't a big deal. "I, umm, I understand. I hope you enjoy," I managed to say without imploding.

And then I got sprayed with water again. I turned around and scanned the backyard, confused. I turned back to the girls and said, "Why do I keep getting wet?" The words were barely out of my mouth when I got sprayed again.

Sammie took that as an opportunity to end an awkward conversation. "I still have a lot to do. I'll see you two in a bit." She turned and hustled back inside.

I looked at Sophie. She said, "I was going to warn you. Sorry, I just found out. Don't be mad at her. She does really like him."

"I know. But he makes me want to puke."

"Me, too, but it's her birthday."

"I tried my best."

"It was fine," Sophie said, peeking around me and then smirking.

"What's the matter?"

"I just saw Love Puddle walk back to the stage over there. Randy has some sort of water pistol in his back pocket."

"Of course he does. I've tried to avoid trouble, but I don't think this is ever going to end."

"What are you going to do?" Sophie asked, concerned.

"Get revenge," I said, in the deepest possible voice.

THE PARTY WAS in full swing. Ditzy Dayna had arrived, as had Ben, Luke, Just Charles, Melody Vonn, Mara Mooney, Jay Parnell, Kieran Murphy, and Cheryl Van Snoogle-Something. There were others, but are you really keeping track?

The sun was long gone. It was time for the best or worst part of the party, depending on who you were. And I was me, so given my relationship with Randy, the Love Puddle performance was gonna be the worst.

Love Puddle's manager stepped up onto the top of the

deck, which was acting as a stage. They didn't even have a real stage, I mean, come on.

The man was in his thirties or forties with a black suit, skinny tie, and sneakers. Total dork move. He stood in front of a keyboard player, drummer, and a guitarist. Randy was nowhere to be seen. "The lights, please," the man said.

The outdoor lights cut out. One spotlight powered on, encasing the man on the stage.

"Ladies and gentlemen, and a special birthday girl, Sammie, please welcome to the stage, the up-and-coming stars, and future winner of... Battle of the Bands. I give you, Love Puddle!"

The crowd rushed to the front of the deck/stage, erupting into hysterics. That is, except for Sophie, me and the rest of my crew. The music kicked in. Nick DeRozan, an obnoxious and quite large football player was banging on the drums so hard, I thought they would pop. The guitarist was strumming away and the keyboardist's fingers were flying across the keys, but there was no Randy. The center of the stage was empty, except for the mic stand. Everyone was looking around for Randy, confused.

And then Randy's voice boomed from the speakers on the sides of the stage. But there was still no sign of him. Confusion spread throughout the crowd. I heard something above us. I turned and looked up. My eyes bulged as Randy Warblemacher walked, no, danced across the roof of Sammie's house. He was literally rocking the house.

"He's on the roof!" Cheryl Van Snoogle-Something shrieked.

The crowd turned around, in awe of what was taking place. Randy sang, "Hey girl, I heard your mamma don't like me."

I yelled out, "Nobody does."

I got a few death stares, but oh, well. It was on. He shouldn't have messed with me, tried to steal Sophie from me during the school year, started a band, or entered Battle of the Bands.

Randy continued, "Well, guess what? I don't like her much, either. Oh, and check this."

Wendy Grier, a known Randy worshiper, yelled out, "Marry me, Randy! Please!"

You can't make this stuff up, folks.

Randy spun around and sang, "Your grandma's an old geezer. I ain't no people pleaser." His high-pitched shrill killed at least three birds that I saw with my own eyes. But the girls seemed to love it.

Thankfully, the song appeared to be winding down. Randy sang a few more lines that made no sense, and then tiptoed to the end of the roof. He reached back with the microphone in his hand and let it fly. It spun in a perfect spiral, hurdling over the pool and the crowd, en route to Love Puddle's oversized drummer, Nick DeRozan. Nick reached up and grabbed it with one hand, nearly crushing it.

To make matters more ridiculous, Randy tore off his shirt, threw it to Sammie, and jumped off the one-story roof (Don't try that at home). The crowd screamed, some scared, some excited. Randy soared over the deck and cannon-balled into the pool. Sammie's parents screamed something to Love Puddle's manager about not having enough insurance.

Randy surfaced to more screams and cheers. As much as I hated him, it was impressive. Still, he was a major show-off.

Randy grabbed a towel out of his manager's hand, dried off, and then put a t-shirt on. I just shook my head. And then I read his t-shirt. It was a Love Puddle shirt!

AFTER THE CONCERT, we were all just hanging out by the pool. Randy walked past me with a few groupies on his heels. He looked at me and smirked.

I couldn't help myself. "Wearing your own band's t-shirt? Who does that?" I asked.

Randy looked at me and said, "You're boring me. Sometimes your mouth moves and I just wish it would stop. Actually, all the time."

"Oh, Randy, you're a hard person not to want to slap... with a shovel. And not one of those plastic beach shovels. Like a real metal shovel. But I'm better than that," I said. "I think."

"So, what's your band name, Austin and the Davenfarts?"

I was surprised. Not by the insult, but because Randy called me Davenfart so often I wasn't sure that he even knew my first name.

"We're Bacon Cheeseburger," I said as cool as I could.

Randy burst out laughing, doubling over at the waist. I didn't think it was that funny. Or funny at all.

"Are you finished?" I asked, annoyed.

"One more minute," Randy said through laughter. After a moment, he stood upright and said, "Okay. I'm good. I didn't know you were so funny."

"I wasn't trying to be funny. You should know. We joined Battle of the Bands. We're gonna win the whole thing. Get ready to be crushed." I wasn't sure where the confidence came from. Our band was terrible.

"Incoming!" Nick DeRozan yelled.

Randy and I both looked toward Nick, eyes wide. Ben, Just Charles, and Luke all rushed forward, Super Soakers locked and loaded. A red liquid burst from the giant water pistols, blasting Randy in the face and his egotistical t-shirt. Randy tried to block the unstoppable force with his hands, but the blasts were, well, unstoppable as described, and continued to pummel him.

Once the unstoppable force stopped, due to lack of fruit punch, Randy wiped his eyes and said, "What the heck was that for?"

"Oh, sorry," Ben said. "We thought you liked puddles."

"Actually, loved them," I said.

"To your face," Ben said. He looked at me, frowning.

And then Randy took off running. Not because we scared him or he was too embarrassed to face the world, but because a swarm of bugs, apparently looking for some sweet dessert, thought that Randy's new layer of fruit punch was it.

"Ahhhhh!" Randy yelled as he sprinted from the backyard.

We all laughed. "That was very satisfying," I said, nearly through tears.

I looked at Ben. He wasn't cracking up like the rest of us. "What's the matter?" I asked. It was a big victory.

"I should've thought of the love puddle, man. I said, 'you like puddles.' I'm not happy."

"I thought you were setting me up."

"No, I missed it. I'll never forgive myself," he said, finally joining the laughter.

10

Our band stood behind a fairly large stage at the center of the Plum Creek Outlets. It was just the five of us. Brody stood off to the side talking to someone who looked somewhat official.

"We gotta crush this. We've been practicing hard. It's all gonna start to come together here." I said, more confidently than I actually was. I just wanted to stick it to Love Puddle ever since Sammie had them play at her party instead of us. It was definitely the right move. They were better than us.

"Should we crush them...or splash them?" Ben asked. He looked at me, expectantly.

"Nice one, Ben." He was working on his puns and quips, ever since he missed the like/love puddle thing.

And then Brody walked over, a big ball of sunshine as always. "I hate to bring you the bad news, but we need a band name," Brody said. "I can't introduce you guys as Bacon Cheeseburger. This is a real gig."

It was a real gig. We were playing at an outlet center, a premium one at that, not for a bunch of squirrels outside Brody's garage.

"Anybody have any ideas?" Brody asked.

We all just shook our heads. I was half expecting Luke to throw out something related to lighting farts again. Lucky for us, he didn't.

"Okay, it's Bacon Cheeseburger then," Brody said, walking away and scratching his head.

After Brody was done talking, I pulled Ben to the side and asked, "How are you feeling?"

"Not so great," he said, looking down at the ground. "I don't know why I get so nervous."

"I do, too. You just gotta do it anyway." I didn't know what else to say. I wasn't a fear expert, and I didn't suffer from it like he did. I could still function, even though I was scared at times. Ben's body just shut down. He went full statue.

"It's just, when I see all those people out there, I freeze."

"Hmmm," I said, looking at Ben's bandana around his neck. We were a little more fashionably coordinated at that point, but it still wasn't pretty.

"What are you thinking?"

"I'm thinking that if you don't like seeing all those people, I'll make them go away."

"Like magic?" Ben asked, excitedly.

"Yep, like magic." I grabbed Ben's bandana and wiggled it from around his neck up to his eyes. I straightened it, making sure he couldn't see out of either one.

"How do you feel?"

"Blind," Ben said.

"Okay. I meant about playing now. Do you think it'll block out the nerves?"

"I think so. I just hope I can play."

"You know where the drums are. You know the songs. What do you need to see for?"

Ben thought about it silently for a moment. I had no idea if any of what I said made any sense, but it sounded good. Kinda.

"All right, gather 'round," the familiar voice of Mr. Muscalini called out.

I walked over to form a musical huddle of sorts. Mr. Muscalini was going to use his master motivational skills to get us pumped up for the show.

Mr. Muscalini began, "Now, I know you guys are nervous. Everybody has nerves. When I played in the Super Bowl I wanted to puke. Even these monstrous quads couldn't stop my knees from shaking. So, I put my helmet on, my mouth piece in, pulled my visor down and hoped to God I didn't puke in my helmet."

"You were in the Super Bowl?" Just Charles asked. "That's soccer, right?"

"Football!" Mr. Muscalini looked up into the sky as he often did when dealing with us nerds. He refocused and answered Just Charles' first question. "Yes. I was the backup to the backup kicker. I was the third foot. They called me 'The Mus'. You know, like the hulking animal. My mother still calls me that. My point is, you feel the fear and you do it anyway. You fake it, til you make it. You may be a bunch of nerds trying to play music, but act like rock stars!"

"Let's do this!" Luke yelled.

"Now bring it in," Mr. Muscalini said.

"We're not going to do a high five are we?" I asked.

"I didn't think you guys even knew what that was," Mr. Muscalini said. "No, I want those hands here in a pile. Bacon Cheeseburger on three. One. Two. Three!"

We all yelled, "Bacon Cheeseburger!"

It felt weird, but it was better than screaming about litter boxes and outhouses, and don't get me started on Luke and his stuff.

"There's one thing left to do," Mr. Muscalini said, stepping toward me.

I wasn't sure what was going on. He grabbed my shirt and arms around my wrists and lifted them up. He stared down each arm, inspecting the angles or perhaps fabric patterns.

"What are you doing, sir?" I asked.

"I'm your new fashion consultant."

"Huh?"

"But you think mesh shirts are a good idea," Luke said.

"The Mus knows fashion," Mr. Muscalini said, simply.

Mr. Muscalini went back to focusing on my shirt or arms or whatever he was doing. He grabbed the edge of my shirt with an iron-clad grip and pulled. The arms of my shirt ripped clean off at the shoulders! I stood there with my naked arms and a dumbfounded look on my face.

"There. Much better. You know the drill, Davenport. Sun's out. Guns out. Let me see you flex."

"I, umm, don't want to do that," I said.

"Come on, just one flex," he said.

"Okay," I said, as I flexed my bicep as hard as I could. I felt the muscle burn and thought it might pop. It had been months since I used my bicep. Nerds barely use their arms.

"When you're ready, Davenport," Mr. Muscalini said.

"I'm flexing!"

"Yeah?" Mr. Muscalini said as he leaned down to get a closer look. "You tracking your protein consumption?"

"Umm, not really."

Mr. Muscalini just shook his head. "Anyway, what do you guys think of his new look?"

"Meh," Sly said.

Everyone else nodded in agreement.

"Yeah, I agree," Mr. Muscalini said. "Bad move, Davenport. I don't know what you're trying to accomplish there, but it ain't working."

"But you did it!"

"That's questionable." Mr. Muscalini handed me the ripped sleeves. "I don't know how they got into my hands, but you might want to hold onto them."

"Thanks," I said with a smirk.

Brody looked at his watch and said, "Okay, time to go. "Follow me."

We walked up the stairs at the back of the stage. I stopped with Ben near the drums. I fixed the bandana over his eyes and said, "Go get 'em, tiger!" I smacked him on the arm and headed over to the microphone.

And then I heard the cymbal nearly explode, followed by a giant splat on the stage. I looked back to see Ben pulling himself up to his knees. Oops. I guess I should've waited until he sat down to put the bandana on.

"I'm okay!" Ben yelled. I wondered why he was yelling so loud. He couldn't see, but his ears were fine.

I gave the thumbs up to Brody who pulled the curtain open. I stood with the mic in my hands and the crowd in front of us was slowly revealed. There were dozens of people, maybe close to a hundred. I was a little nervous, but I knew once the music started, I would be okay.

And then the music began. I wished it hadn't. Ben's crash was foreshadowing for our entire performance. It started off just fine. We got into a little groove. The crowd was swaying back and forth or playing on their phones. I checked behind me and Ben seemed to be okay. He wasn't frozen solid, so that was a plus.

A few kids held their hands above the edge of the stage.

Things were going well, so I did my version of dancing over to them. It was probably more like Ben's fear waddle, but I did my best. I leaned down to slap some fives. I should've known better. Even when their hands weren't moving, I had trouble connecting on the five. I reached for one, leaned too far, missed the five, and slipped on the edge of the platform. I fell flat on my butt, the momentum causing me to fall to my back.

I sang from the floor of the stage as I lay there, hoping the crowd thought it was part of my rock star entertainment. That was not the case. I heard some laughter and even some boos, which didn't feel too good. I rolled over, stood up, and continued singing. I scanned the crowd for the booers and my heart sunk to my stomach. Love Puddle was in the crowd and seemingly leading the charge in revolt.

I needed to win the rest of the crowd back. I needed to engage them. We were heading up to the hook that everybody in the crowd would know, so I yelled into the mic, "Everybody sing!"

I held the mic out for the crowd to sing. Nothing. Well, it was worse than nothing. I heard Love Puddle yell, "Get off the stage!" It echoed throughout the speaker system. More laughter.

Behind me, things weren't much better. Ben was off beat, which meant that Luke was, too. I looked at Sly. He was not happy. But we had bigger problems. The boos were growing in size and decibels. I sang louder to try to drown out the crowd, but was knocked off course as something soft and squishy connected with the side of my head.

I looked down to see a splattered tomato on the stage. I looked out at the crowd and saw nothing but red. That one tomato opened the floodgates. Seemingly bushels of tomatoes soared through the sky, pelting me, Sly, and Just

Charles. Luke was ducking behind Ben, who continued to play, not having any idea of what was happening, given that he was wearing the bandana over his eyes.

Thankfully or perhaps, mercifully, Brody and the security guard pulled the curtain closed with fury. To add insult to injury, I looked through the closing curtain to see Randy launch a tomato behind a wicked smile that caused me to freeze just like the Beef Stroganoff incident on my first day in middle school. It connected with my forehead, knocking me back. I fell on my butt and slid across the floor, hating Randy. And tomatoes.

11

The security guard ushered us to a secure area inside an unoccupied store. The windows were blacked out and there were no tomatoes in sight. Mr. Muscalini was with us while Brody did damage control with the outlet's management.

We tried to clean ourselves off, wiping tomatoes out of our hair and wringing out our shirts.

"Hey, don't waste that!" Mr. Muscalini said. "That's fresh tomato juice. It's about time for a smoothie."

I ignored him and said, "Who the heck brings tomatoes to a rock concert?"

The security guard chimed in. "There was a farmer's market going on at the other side of the outlets. Saturdays from 11-3."

"You really gonna drink this?" Sly asked, holding his tomato-drenched shirt.

Mr. Muscalini said, "Hey, man. I like fresh produce just as much as the next guy. Just because I eat a lot of protein doesn't mean I don't need my veggies, too."

"I got hit with some lady's shoe," Luke said, holding the actual old lady shoe.

Jus Charles said, "Sorry. I think that's my Nana's."

"Well, she's going down. Reverse Cinderella style. I'm gonna shove that shoe on every old lady's foot until it fits and then we fight," Luke said.

"I just told you it was my Nana's, idiot. And she'll crush you. But still, sorry."

"It's not your Nana's fault. Randy started it," I said. "He was in the crowd. He threw at least two tomatoes at me."

"Didn't you guys learn anything from dodgeball? You got pummeled. Wait, Randy? Warblemacher?"

"Yes," I said.

"Were his throws accurate?" Mr. Muscalini asked.

"Yes, why?"

"I'm thinking I should recruit him to pitch next baseball season." He turned to Just Charles. "How's your Nana's curve ball?"

"What does this all matter?" Sly asked, angrily. "It was terrible out there!"

"Yeah, it was mayhem!" Just Charles yelled.

"I'm so mad!" Luke yelled.

Mr. Muscalini said, "Okay, men! In hindsight, calling yourselves Bacon Cheeseburger during the tomato festival was probably not a good idea."

"Wait a minute. Mayhem. Mad. Men." I looked at the rest of the crew. "I've got a new band name! We're the Mayhem Mad Men!"

"I love it!" Brody said.

The crew all agreed. After we did a mini celebration (no high-fives), I could tell Ben was still upset.

We walked over to the side. Ben asked, "Why does this

always happen to me? Why can't I be a normal kid? I can't talk to girls, give a speech, play in a band."

"Did you see the rest of us?"

"No, you blindfolded me."

"That's probably a good thing. We were terrible and me, especially. I actually fell down on the stage."

Brody interrupted, "Okay, guys. Let's pretend that never happened."

"Shouldn't we try to learn something from this?" Just Charles asked.

"Oh, of course. I didn't mean that. I think we've learned that...we should...well, umm, Just Charles' Nana has a good arm," Brody said, shrugging. "This has been fun, but I've been told we need to vacate the premises immediately and we are not to return until we are full-grown adults."

"Even me?" Mr. Muscalini asked.

"You're not in the band, so I'm thinking, no," Brody answered. "On a positive note, they were expecting it to be a record day in tomato sales at the farmers market."

THAT MONDAY, I got dropped off at camp with Leighton, which meant that we were a little earlier than the bus and the rest of the kids. I plopped down on a tree stump waiting for the other kids in my group to arrive. I was still bummed about our performance.

I heard footsteps approaching. I looked up to see Teddy. I nodded as he plopped down next to me.

"You okay?" he asked.

"My band bombed over the weekend. We got pelted with tomatoes."

"Oh, that sounds bad. Were they rotten?"

"No," I said, annoyed.

"So, I guess it could've been worse," Teddy said, shrugging.

"I guess so." I thought about it for the moment. "We did come up with our band name there."

"Cool. What is it?"

"The Mayhem Mad Men," I said, proudly. Well, I was proud of the name. We stunk as a band, but like everyone said, as long as you had a good name, you were in solid shape.

"That's awesome. What's next?"

"Keep practicing, I guess. Somehow Brody got us another gig. Maybe we can redeem ourselves. I just hope he's smart enough to book somewhere without perishables."

"When's your next gig? Maybe I'll come."

"We just sold out Vintage Retirement Community," I said, shrugging.

"Really? My Nana is there. I'll definitely go and see you guys."

"How's your Nana's arm?" I asked.

Teddy laughed. "Don't worry, I think you'll be fine there."

I shrugged. "We'll see." He hadn't seen Just Charles' Nana toss a shoe at us. I hoped Just Charles' Nana didn't live with Teddy's. And that she was an outlier in the old lady community. If all the old bags at the VRC had arms like hers, we weren't gonna make it out of there alive.

WE PRACTICED REALLY HARD the next few days. We were definitely getting better. But Ben was still in crisis. He had no confidence in himself. He was still frustrated by how his fear just kicked in and there was nothing he could do to stop it.

As we walked into gardens at the retirement center, all of the residents had already gathered. I smiled at an old lady with a walker. And then I looked down in horror. She had tennis balls attached to the bottom of her walker. I pretended not to see anything. I didn't need Ben or any of the others worrying about getting pummeled again.

We quickly set up our equipment. Our fans were dropping like flies. A bunch of people were already asleep while a handful of others were scattered around on the ground after falling. One lady at the front of a line fell backward, knocking down a crew of oldies, one by one.

I looked over at Ben while he assembled his drum set. His face was filled with angst. I walked over to him.

"Hey, what's going on?" I asked. "How are you feeling?"

"I don't know. My stomach feels like a war zone."

"Dude," I said, nonchalantly. "This doesn't even matter. They're so old, they probably can't even hear us." I pointed out to the growing crowd. "I mean, look at that one. You can't bore him. He's already asleep. Or dead. He might be dead. Should we tell someone?"

"True," Ben said, thinking, apparently not caring that there was a dead dude in the crowd.

"Do you want to wear my Beats headphones? I have them in my bag. With the bandana and them, you won't be able to hear or see anything."

"Yeah, let's try that," Ben said, nodding.

When we were ready to play, I sat Ben on his stool this time to avoid another crash and then put on the bandana. Once that was covering his eyes, I put the headphones on.

"How is he going to know when to start?" Sly asked.

"Good point," I said, thinking.

Just Charles kicked the drum and then Ben screamed out, "One, two, three!" And we kicked off our next performance, as I scrambled up to the microphone to entertain the masses of the Vintage Retirement Community.

Everything was going well until I saw an old lady stand up in the back of the crowd. She held not one, but two shoes above her head. I thought we were in for it. I slid over to a tree and sang while peeking out from behind it.

And then she disappeared. I looked out as I continued singing. All of a sudden, I saw both shoes fly up into the air. I shuddered, but realized she threw them behind her, and then reappeared on the shoulders of an old man! And then they were gone again, both of them crashing to the ground. A worker rushed to them.

The crowd wasn't moving. Half of them were sprawled out on the ground. Was it because we were boring or maybe we killed them? I didn't think we were that bad, so I continued on.

We finished our set. We didn't get a standing ovation. In our defense, most of them were in wheelchairs, but we did get a few claps and cheers. And nobody threw tomatoes, so that was a huge plus.

After the performance, Teddy ran over to us. "I loved it! You guys were awesome."

"Thanks, man. I'm just glad nobody threw anything."

Teddy pointed across the room to his Nana. "That's my Nana over there. I want you to meet her."

I furrowed my brow and asked, "What's she wearing?"

"Don't worry. She can't reach her shoes."

"I was talking about her glasses."

"Oh. She just had glaucoma surgery. It protects her eyes from the light."

Ben asked, "She was in a coma?"

"No, it's an eye thing," Teddy said, laughing.

"Come on, guys. I'll introduce you."

We followed Teddy through the maze of wheelchairs and walkers. It was difficult because some of them were moving at a mile an hour. Nana sat on a concrete bench next to a rose garden. It seemed like a big risk to have thorny roses everywhere with old people falling like dominos around the clock. Nana had a sweet, wrinkly face, nearly half of it engulfed by the oversized sunglasses, and short silver hair.

"Hello, grandson!" She looked at Ben and me. "And what a wonderful performance you had."

Teddy said, "Nana, this is Austin and Ben, my friends from camp."

Nana put out her hand for a shake. She nearly crushed my hand. She must've been hitting the gym with Mr. Muscalini. I was glad I hadn't met her before the performance. Had I known she was that strong, I would've been nervous that she could throw a boulder in my direction.

"It's nice to meet you," I said.

"Likewise," Nana said, with a smile.

"Do you think everyone liked the performance?" I asked, nervously.

"Oh, yes. We are quite the Rock 'n Roll fans here. Gertrude over there once kissed a Beatle."

"Why would she kiss a bug? That's just disgusting," Ben said.

"No, dude. She meant, 'The Beatles', the famous band from England." My parents loved them.

Nana chuckled and then said, "You know, the girls and I were talking and we think it behooves you to wear leather pants when you perform."

"Behooves?" Ben asked.

"It's in your interest," Nana said, laughing.

"We'll take that under consideration." I wasn't sure leather pants were for me. I didn't know if I was cool enough to pull that off.

Nana looked at Ben and said, "And you, young man, that was very impressive, playing the drums while blindfolded. The best entertainers have showmanship."

Ben smiled from ear to ear. "Thank you."

I was happy he got some praise for his performance. He needed it.

"I want you guys for my bar mitzvah," Teddy said.

"Really? Why?" I asked without thinking.

Teddy laughed. "You guys will rock it!"

"I hope so," I said.

Teddy looked at Nana and asked, "What do you think, Nan?"

"I agree. They would rock it!"

"Well, we better clean up our stuff. It was nice meeting you," I said to Nana.

"Good luck, boys!"

As we walked away, I said to Ben, "I think you've been hanging out with Ditzy Dayna too much."

"I have not. I'm just stressed, man. I just want to be better."

"Nana said you did great."

"Yeah, but she's old," Ben said, moping.

"Don't worry. I think I have an idea," I said, mysteriously.

12

The morning after our gig at the Vintage Retirement Community, which the VRC newsletter called, 'Riveting' and said, 'The lead singer had the ladies falling all over themselves.' I sat in the den trying to figure out how to be better. Sure, we rocked a retirement home, but we weren't convinced they actually heard any of it. And maybe the bar was set low. We had to be better than Bingo! We didn't give out any prizes, though, so maybe not.

Leighton walked in and plopped down next to me, eating a granola bar, and threw a plastic shopping bag on the coffee table. "What's up, punk?" she asked.

"Trying to figure out how to make our band better."

"I have just the thing. Open up that bag."

I furrowed my brow as I reached for the bag. I grabbed it and opened it. I reached my hand in and felt the material inside. It was smooth and cool. I pulled it out to reveal a pair of black leather pants.

"It's faux leather, but nobody has to know that," she said. "Camp Cherriwacka doesn't pay enough for real leather."

"An old lady told me I should have leather pants. It's sad that an old lady knows more about rocking out than I do."

Leighton laughed. "Try them on. It'll make you look like a real rock star."

"I need all the help I can get. Thanks. I'm gonna try these suckers out next time I'm up on stage." That was a mistake, but I didn't know it at the time. Of course, I didn't try them on first. Hey, I'm a kid. That's what we do. We don't do what people tell us to do.

So, do you want the good news or the bad news? Or both? Okay. The good news is that Randy didn't show up at our next performance and embarrass us, and no more old ladies were harmed in the telling of this story. Well, not yet, anyway. I make no promises about what's to come. The bad news is that I embarrassed our crew all on my own. Here's what happened.

Our next gig was in full swing. We were crushing a kindergarten graduation party. The kids were running around like crazy as we played. True, they had been pumped full of sugar for the previous two hours, but we were awesome. Ben was on time with the music, which meant that Luke was too and kept Sly from being angry at Ben.

And then it happened. As I did a monstrous Kung-Fu kick, I felt my faux pants stretch to their limits. I thought I was fine, but I heard the kids screaming louder than usual.

"Ewww!" The graduate yelled. "I see his butt crack!"

No! The faux leather failed me! I reached behind me and felt the back of my pants. They were torn the entire length of my butt crack! My heart pounded as I instinctively turned back around, away from the crowd. But because I am a professional, I continued singing while squeezing my butt cheeks together. It's hard. I'm pretty certain that if I had the courage to tell my music teacher, Mrs. Funderbunk, she would be very proud.

I looked back at the band and Just Charles was cracking up behind me, no pun intended. Luke and Sly joined in. I was glad that Ben was wearing the bandana so at least there was one person at the party who didn't see my butt.

Now, you might be asking, "How did the birthday kid see Austin's butt crack if he was wearing underwear?" And the answer is that nobody wears underwear with leather pants. If you ever see someone wearing leather pants, ask them. Until then, you'll just have to believe me.

Thankfully, that was our last song. Surprisingly, we didn't get a tip from the birthday kid's parents. Not sure why not...

THE NEXT DAY AT CAMP, I was still mad. I know it wasn't anyone's fault, but I blamed it on Leighton and Teddy's Nana. And now that I think about it, I also blame the manufacturer. Yes, I should've tried the pants on first, but leather pants are supposed to be tight. And I didn't see any warnings on the labels that said, 'No flying Kung-Fu kicks while wearing these poorly-made faux leather pants.' I mean, who wears leather pants besides rock stars? They should know we're going to do crazy stuff in them. And reinforcements in the butt crack area would've been nice, too.

I walked into the pool area and past Leighton and just shook my head. I didn't have to say a word.

"Leather pants are supposed to be tight," she said, defensively.

"Tell that to the dozens of kindergarteners who were traumatized by my butt crack."

"You're such a drama king," Leighton said, laughing.

"You wouldn't think it was so funny if it was your butt crack," I said.

"True, but it wasn't mine." Leighton continued laughing.

I was mad, but distracted by a tall man wearing a cleaning uniform.

"Zorch?" I asked.

The man turned around. A smile registered on his face when he saw me. "Austin! How are you, buddy?"

"You're friends with Zorch?" Leighton asked, shocked. "The custodian from Cherry Avenue?"

"Yeah," I said, as Zorch walked over to us. He was one of my best friends. He helped me save the Halloween dance in sixth grade.

"What are you doing here?" I asked.

"The camp needed a facilities manager for the summer, so here I am."

"Awesome!"

Leighton chimed in, "Hey, Zorch. Austin's in a band and we're having a disagreement. You're really old- you know Rock 'n Roll, right?"

"Hey! I'm forty two!"

Leighton looked at Zorch, confused. "Yeah, that's really old, isn't it?"

Zorch shook his head. "What's the disagreement?"

"If you split a pair of leather pants while performing, it's nobody's fault but your own, right? I mean, you should know the risks of wearing leather pants."

"Yeah, but nobody told me those risks," I said.

Zorch laughed. "Sounds like you had a wardrobe malfunction. Sorry, Aus. They come with the territory. I have to agree with your sister here."

"I thought you were my friend," I said, with a smirk.

Things didn't get better from there. As I was heading back to my group, Sly met me halfway.

"I gotta show you something," Sly said, smiling. He pulled out his phone and pulled up YouTube.

"Okay, what is it?" I asked.

"A video of a friend of mine," Sly said, pressing play.

The video was a close-up of a middle school kid, rocking out on the drums. He was amazing. His hands moved like lightning from drum to drum. And that was just the warm up. He built up into a crescendo, his hands moving so fast I could barely keep up with them. He ended with a giant blast of the cymbal. It vibrated as he threw his arms into the air with a primal scream.

"That was amazing," I said. "He's like a superstar."

"I knew you would say that," Sly said. "One million views. He lives just one town over. He's looking for a band to play with."

"Okay," I said, unsure of what he was getting at. "Maybe Brody can help him."

"I was thinking for us. For Mayhem Mad Men," Sly said, eyeing me.

"But, Ben-"

Sly cut me off. "Ben's holding us back. We can be something. People will finally give you respect. Don't you want that?"

"Yes, but he's my best friend."

"That's fine," Sly said, "But he shouldn't be our drummer."

13

I couldn't sleep that night. I didn't want to believe what Sly told me. That Ben wasn't good enough to be our drummer, but part of me knew it was true. He was getting better, but we basically had to lock him up in a padded room and were never gonna win Battle of the Bands with the way he was playing. And if we couldn't play well, we were never gonna be cool. I realized there was a flaw in Cameron Quinn's system. Being in a band gave a certain level of street cred until people see you play. The band name helps, but rocking an old age home didn't make us cool. We needed people our own age to think it was cool.

I thought about whether or not we could just tell people we were in a band, but never actually play a gig, at least until we graduated from high school. I wasn't sure that would work. But the rest of us weren't that much better, to be honest. I couldn't give up on him. And I still wanted to try out the idea I got from Nana's glaucoma shades.

Sly met me first thing in the morning as we all made our way into camp. Ben, Luke, and Just Charles continued on without us as I hung back to talk.

The first thing he said was, "Did you think about it?"

"I did. I don't want to kick him out. I have an idea to try first," I said.

"What?" he asked, frustrated.

"Blinders," I said, as we walked toward the common area.

"Blinders? Like on race horses?" Sly asked, confused. "He already wears a bandana over his eyes."

"No, not race horses. Old people."

"Huh?" Sly said as we joined the others.

"He needs to feel cool. I'll tell you more later. I think it could work."

Before Sly could protest, Brody ushered our band away from the crowd and said, "Okay, shut your faces and good morning." We all quieted down before Brody continued, "I've been thinking about why we stink."

"We stink?" Just Charles asked.

"Where the heck have you been?" I asked.

Brody answered, "Yes, we stink. But I have the answer. We need that It Factor. That thing that makes us unique. That gives us the edge. Anybody can do weak covers, man. You gotta come up with something original. If we're gonna make it to the big time, we gotta write our own songs."

I stood up and said, "There's only one thing we can do."

"What's that?"

"A songwriting sleepover."

"I'm out," Sly said. "I don't do songwriting sleepovers."

"How many have you been invited to?" I asked.

"This is the first one, but I've always had this rule."

"How is that possible? I think this is the first songwriting sleepover ever," I said.

"It's not. Prince had them all the time," Sly said.

"Who the heck is Prince?" Ben asked.

"He's the greatest guitarist of all time!" Sly said, a little too aggressively. Granted, the songwriting sleepover was revolutionary and beyond important, but we didn't have to start getting crazy over it.

If it was good enough for Prince, why not us?

"Oh, you're on a first name basis now with the greatest guitarist of all time?" Just Charles asked.

Sly smirked. "Prince didn't have a last name, did he?"

"Oh, yeah."

"Still, I said he was the greatest guitarist of all time, not songwriter," Sly said, shaking his head

"Okay, we'll figure it out," I said. I had a feeling that Sly was angry at Ben for other reasons, mainly because he thought Ben stunk.

WE HAD the songwriting sleepover at my house. Sly refused to come. I was pretty angry. Yeah, he was super cool and a great guitarist, but we were barely friends. We had just met a few weeks ago and he was asking me to kick my best friend out of the band.

I had gathered everything we needed for a productive songwriting sleepover: pizza, chips, pretzels, and sugary soda. Oh, and my iPad to write down or record the lyrical masterpieces that were going to flow from our collective minds.

The band, minus Sly, was holed up in my basement with our plentiful supplies. Brody had tried to get himself invited to the sleepover, but we felt it was band members only. Plus, we were pretty certain he just wanted to hang out with my sister.

We sat around on the couch and a few beanbag chairs I

had brought down from my room. I asked the crew, "What should we write about?"

Luke said, "I don't know, lighting farts?"

Just Charles said, "Bacon?"

"Really? We're going back there?" I asked.

Luke shrugged. "That's all I'm good at."

"Lighting farts?" Ben asked.

"Yeah, you wanna see?"

Ben and I yelled a collective, "No!"

Just Charles looked at Luke and asked, "What are you thinking about lyrics?"

"Why are you even considering this?" I questioned.

Luke ignored me, put his pointer finger on his ear like a professional singer and went into full on rock star mode. He sang, "I light my farts in the dark." He looked at our unconvinced faces and said, "We could make it a rap?" And then, unfortunately, he rapped, "I light my farts and I cannot lie!" If you don't know why that's funny, ask your parents.

"No. Just no," I said.

Luke paused and then said, "Or it could be a love song." He sang, "Come on baby, light my fart!"

"That's terrible," I said.

"Yeah, man." Ben said. "That's something Love Puddle would do."

"Maybe I'll sell it to them."

"I would actually pay to see Randy sing about lighting farts," I said to laughter.

"What would you do?" Luke asked me.

"I would make it less bad."

"Yeah, that's helpful."

Just Charles chimed in, "Should we ask Brody what he thinks?"

"Couldn't hurt," Ben said.

"That's not entirely accurate," I said, "but we need something better than this."

"That's rude," Luke said.

"Sorry, not sorry," I said as I grabbed my phone and hit Brody up on FaceTime.

"Mad Men! You create any mayhem yet?" Brody said, his face too close to the phone.

"No, but it looks pretty crazy up your nose," I said.

"Oh, sorry." He pulled the phone back.

"We can't think of anything," Ben said.

"Not true," Luke responded.

"Anything good," I corrected.

Luke punched me.

"Owww!" I said, rubbing my arm.

"Whoa, dudes. You can't get frustrated. This is what I've learned from French Lisp. You gotta write what you know, man. Write life."

Ben looked at the rest of us and said, "What the heck do we know?"

"Wheels on the bus was already done," Just Charles said.

Brody was looking around like somehow by changing his angles, he would be able to see behind us.

"Your sister back there?" Brody asked, craning his neck.

"No, she's waiting for you at Burger Boy!" I said.

"What? I gotta go, dudes!" And like that, Brody was gone.

"Oops," I said. "I hope he figures out I was kidding. But he kinda deserves it. Well, let's get back to it."

"What do we know?" Ben asked again.

"Nothing," Luke said. He cracked open a soda and took a sip.

"Middle School," Just Charles said.

"Middle school stinks," Ben said.

"No, it's mayhem," I corrected. "That's it. That's what we sing about!"

"What?" Ben asked.

"About how crazy middle school is," I said, excited.

"Yes!" Ben yelled.

"I love it," Just Charles said, scarfing down some pretzels.

"It's okay," Luke said to stares. "Okay, it's really good," he said, smiling.

"What stinks about middle school?" Ben asked.

"What's crazy about it?" I followed.

"6 A.M. wake ups," Just Charles answered.

"Too much body spray, perfume and makeup," Luke rhymed.

I added on, "History's a mystery, foreign language is pure misery."

Ben sang, "Field trips to landfills and fire drills."

"Study hall, dodge ball, why can't we just chill?" Just Charles sang.

I took it home, "Middle School Mayhem! Parent's think we're learning, but they don't got a clue." I looked at Just Charles. "Can you write the music?" I asked, excitedly.

"Absolutely!" Just Charles popped up. We all followed.

"This is gonna be a huge hit!" I yelled.

I reached back excitedly and thrust my hand up for a high-five. All of our hands missed, causing our arms to get tangled in a giant knot. It took a minute or two to get untangled, but it didn't dampen our spirit. Mayhem Mad Men was about to take off!

14

Even though I was mad that Sly didn't come to our songwriting sleepover, I couldn't wait to sing the song for him. I hoped it would cause him to ease up on getting rid of Ben. With a hit new song, he might forget about his replacement idea.

The next time we had camp, of course, Brody was nowhere to be found, so we had a chance to play it with Sly. The four of us walked up to him as he sat on one of the old tree stumps, strumming his guitar.

"Wussup, Mad Men. How was the songwriting sleep-over?" he asked, sarcastically.

"It was okay," I pretended. "You know, we may have, possibly, gotten our first hit!" I said.

Just Charles handed Sly some sheet music. "Get a load of this. I was up all night writing it."

Sly took the sheet of music and frowned, skeptically. "Hmm," he said, softly.

"What?" Just Charles asked.

"This might actually be good."

"Actually? Oh, gee. Thanks," Just Charles said, sarcastically.

Sly handed the sheet to Ben and said, "Here. Hold this for me. Let's try it out."

Ben held the music up in front of Sly's face. Sly scanned the page and then played a few chords.

I joined in, singing, "6 A.M. wake ups. Too much body spray, perfume, and make up."

Sly slapped the side of his guitar and stopped playing. We all looked at him, hoping he would like it.

"So, what do you think?" I asked.

Sly furrowed his brow and then broke out into a smile, "I love it! This is gonna rock!"

Brody walked up. "Good news. We've got a new gig, nerds."

"That's unnecessary," I said.

"Sorry. I've been trying to bond with Mr. Muscalini. I think he's rubbing off on me."

"Where's our new gig?" Sly asked.

"A theme park."

"Like Six Flags?" Ben asked.

"Yeah," Brody said, unconvincingly. "But a little bit smaller."

I scratched my head, "How much smaller?"

"Like minus everything except one ride."

"What ride?" Just Charles asked.

Brody whispered, "The carousel."

"The what?" I asked. "Did you say, 'carousel'?"

"Maybe. How do you feel about that?"

"Does it pay?" Luke asked. "I'm only in it for the money."

"We get a cut of the ticket revenue."

"What carousel?" Just Charles asked.

"The one by the beach."

"The carousel at the beach is free!" I yelled.

DESPITE THE MANAGERIAL mishap by our esteemed manager and camp counselor, we played the non-paying gig anyway.

We rocked the carousel. And we figured out a way to make a little dough. Sly put his empty guitar case on the ground out in front of us and a bunch of people tossed in cash. After it was over, we packed up and gathered around Sly.

"How much money did we make?" Luke asked Sly, nodding to the handful of money in his guitar case.

"What do you mean?"

"The money in your case."

"What about it?" Sly asked, confused.

"How much do we each get?"

"You all get zero. I get all of it."

"What are you talking about?"

"It's my case."

Ben stared at Sly. "Are you serious?"

I looked at Sly and said, "Dude, really?"

"Yeah, man," Brody said.

And then my phone rang. I pulled it out of my pocket and answered it. "Hello?" It was Teddy. "Yeah, of course we want to play at your bar mitzvah."

"Whoa, whoa. I'm the manager," Brody said. "I'll handle this."

I covered the phone and whispered excitedly, "He wants to pay us $500."

Brody yelled, "Accept it now!"

I was so excited about the new gig. It made up for the twelve bucks and a half-eaten hot dog we got at our phenomenal performance at the carousel. I couldn't wait to call Sophie.

As soon as she answered, I said, "Hey, just got back from the gig. Nobody threw anything at us, so I'm thinking it was good." It was a low bar to set, but you gotta start somewhere.

"I know. That's so great," Sophie said.

"What do you mean, you know? Were you there? How come I didn't see you?"

"I wish. No, Luke told me."

"Oh. Since when do you talk to Luke on the phone?"

"I don't know. He just called me."

"Weird, but okay. Anyway, I'm looking forward to Teddy's bar mitzvah. It should be a fun gig."

"You guys will do awesome."

I wasn't sure she was right, but I wasn't going to disagree with her.

It was the night of Teddy Katz's bar mitzvah. We had practiced like mad (no pun intended.) We were all set up, so we just sat in an empty room, waiting for the guests to arrive. We were all pretty nervous. Not only were we still an inexperienced band, we were playing in front of a lot of kids we knew. We could be heroes or we could be zeroes. I was a lot more excited when we got the gig than when we got to the gig.

Teddy stuck his long neck and head into the door like a llama checking things out. "Hey, guys! Come get some food. Things are kicking off!"

We followed him out to the party. It was crazy how much food there was everywhere.

"Dude!" Ben said.

He didn't have to say anything else. I knew exactly what he was saying. There were too many food stations to count. There was pasta, steak, sushi, and even Chinese food in little take-out containers. I was so excited that I forgot about the gig for a minute. That is, until I saw Randy.

He was all suited up with shiny shoes and his hair perfectly coiffed, as usual. Regan was by his side, holding his hand, in a blue sequined dress, looking like a movie star or something. Ben took a step back. There wasn't any water around, but you can't be too careful.

"Davenfart! So good to see you. I can't wait to see you guys perform. You guys put on some comedy act."

"Very funny," I said, angrily. "Why are you even here?"

"He's my date," Regan said.

"Since when do you get to bring a date to a bar mitzvah?" Ben asked.

"Since I tell every kid that I'm not going unless I get to bring a guest and get a supreme party favor package of my choosing," Regan said, snottily.

"I think Teddy is sending me to the Bahamas. Or was it Barbados? Or both? I forget."

I looked at Randy and said icily. "You two are perfect for each other." I said to Ben, "Let's get out of here."

"Hey Gordo, remember when you thought Regan would kiss you and then you fell in the pool?" Randy asked, laughing. "Classic Gordo."

"She pushed me!"

"Don't worry about it," I said, pulling Ben away. "We've got a gig to play. And we need to rock it."

We went to the main hall. The band was all set up on

stage. Ben sat in the back with his bandana over his eyes and headphones on. I took a deep breath and nodded to Just Charles. He kicked Ben's drum.

Ben yelled out, "One, two, three!" And then started playing.

It was only the second time we played our new song, "Middle School Mayhem", in front of anyone. And the first time was at the carousel, which meant that most of the people listening only heard like 5% of the song, as they circled around on bobbing horses.

I looked out into the crowd and was nearly blinded. A red light hit my eye so hard that I thought I felt it in the back of my skull. I had no idea what it was. I stumbled, but was able to pull it together in time to start off the song.

"6 A.M. wake up! The halls are filled with too much body spray, perfume, and makeup!" I sang.

I thought it sounded good, so I was shocked when I heard some laughter from the crowd. I looked around as I continued singing and then saw the red light again. It was on Just Charles forehead. He didn't seem to notice. I searched the crowd for Randy, knowing full well he was up to something.

I continued to sing, "Things have never been so clear, you gotta get me outta here! I'm so filled with fear. Who came up with this idea? Middle school mayhem-"

And then the crowd really started to crack up. I looked down to see the red dot on my chest. I covered it with my hand. I know, dumb move. It really didn't cover anything. The light jumped to the other side of my chest. I covered it. The light jumped again, this time to my crotch. I covered it quickly, nearly knocking myself out in the process. The crowd laughed again.

Randy kept popping the light around. I eventually just

gave up and powered through it. I thought about turning around, but I didn't want him lasering my butt in front of everyone. The silver lining in the whole thing was that with all the moving around with the light, my dance moves were better than normal.

When the show was over, Ditzy Dayna ran over to us and shrieked, "I totally love the song!"

"Thanks," I said. "We wrote it together. You know, about life."

"It's like you guys have actually been to our middle school," she said, twirling her hair.

"We are in your school," Ben said, annoyed.

"Yeah, you do look kinda familiar."

"Yeah, I'm Austin Davenport. We've been in school together since kindergarten."

Sophie shook her head, trying not to laugh.

A little boy, maybe six or seven, ran up to us, interrupting our conversation. He looked up at me, his eyes wide.

"Can I have your autograph?"

"Umm, sure," I said. "I don't have anything to sign with."

"My mom gave me a pen." He grabbed the yarmulke off his head and handed it to me. "You can sign this."

"Okay," I said. "You sure?"

"Yeah, my mom said it was okay."

I took the yarmulke and signed it. "Here you go."

"Thanks!" The kid ran away, staring at the autograph like it was his most valued treasure.

I looked at my friends and realized they were trying not to crack up. Once the boy was out of earshot, they didn't hold back. The group exploded with laughter, except Luke. I smiled sheepishly.

"We're famous!" Ben said.

"He's famous," Luke corrected, annoyed.

"What's the matter with you?" I asked.

"Nothing," Luke said, walking away.

15

After the bar mitzvah, despite my new-found fame, we still needed to get better. Brody was off doing some male bonding with Mr. Muscalini (probably smashing bricks with their foreheads or something similarly crazy), so his garage wasn't available. So, practice was going to be at my house. Sophie was there, too. She wanted to see us practice.

Before the whole gang got to my house, I sat in the kitchen with Sophie, drinking chocolate milk and reading comments from the band's Instagram account.

"Listen to this one," I read, "Lead singer rocks "Middle School Mayhem.""

"Don't get sucked into the fame, kid," Sophie said, laughing.

I read some more, "Band is cool. Front man, yeah, that's me, front man, can sing, but has no moves." I dropped my phone on the table. "No moves!"

Leighton walked in as I was having a tantrum.

"That's not wrong," Leighton said.

"Oh, thanks, sis," I said, chugging my milk.

"You're not a singer," she responded.

"Geez, tell me how you really feel."

"That's not what I meant. Let me finish. You're an entertainer. People don't go to a concert to hear music. They download that. They go to a concert to see a show."

"She's right," Sophie said.

"Okay, I understand," I said, nodding my head. "But I thought I at least had some moves."

Sophie pursed her lips. Leighton was suddenly quiet.

"Your silence speaks volumes."

"Don't be mad," Leighton said. "Sophie and I can teach you some moves."

"I have an amazing Kung-Fu kick. I just can't wear faux leather while doing it," I said.

"Don't get started on that again."

"We made $200 on that gig, but had to pay $500 for the birthday boy's therapy after seeing my butt crack."

"Stop it," Leighton said, laughing.

"It doesn't have to be crazy. Baby steps," Sophie said.

"Yeah, like wave your empty hand in a semi-circle above your head as you sing."

"And we'll throw some sunglasses on you or something."

"You need badditude," Leighton said, like I had any idea of what she was talking about.

"Huh?"

"Badditude. It's a bad attitude, but not like mean bad, cool bad," Leighton explained.

"That's not really my style," I said.

"We have to make it your style," Leighton said, simply.

WE HAD BEEN PRACTICING for at least fifteen minutes before

Luke actually showed up. He walked slowly over to us with his bass case in his hand, totally dragging.

"You're late," I said, simply.

"I hate practicing," he said.

"What's the matter with you?" Just Charles said.

"The bass is boring. I don't want to be a bassist."

I was about to call him an idiot, but Sophie took a better approach.

"My dad plays the bass and the guitar. The bass is like the leader- showing the way for the drummer and the rhythm guitar. It's super important."

We all just kind-of stared at her. I didn't know she knew anything about playing music. She had a wonderful singing voice, but we never talked about instruments.

"That's pretty cool," Luke said. "I didn't know that."

Sophie looked down at the ground, "You're just..."

"What?" Luke asked.

"...in need of a more practice," Sophie said, sheepishly.

"And you can do better?" Luke asked, angrily.

Sly chortled. "Girls can't rock out."

"Watch me," Sophie said, confidently.

I looked on with serious interest.

Sophie grabbed the guitar and put the strap over her head. She moved her fingers up and down the bass, seemingly getting familiar with it. She then proceeded to crush "Middle School Mayhem" from memory.

Five jaws dropped open at the same time as she ripped like a pro.

Sophie finished and handed the bass back to Luke. It was basically smoking, she crushed it so hard.

Luke stared at the bass, surprised that it was capable of doing the things that Sophie just did with it.

"That's my girlfriend," I said to Ben. "She rocks."

"Can you teach me how to play like that? I now love the bass. And you," Luke said, laughing.

"Settle down," I said, firmly.

Sly walked over to Sophie and said, "I'm sorry that I said girls can't rock out. I was wrong." He had a look in his eye that I didn't like.

"Don't let it happen again," Sophie said, straight faced. As she turned around, she smiled at me.

It was like the first time I had seen her, all over again, when she floated into science class like an angel. The problem was, I think half the band felt the same way.

16

I sat at the kitchen table eating breakfast with Derek. He was watching Netflix on his phone, so he ignored me, which was better than when he paid attention to me. I was busy writing a new song. Or trying to. I didn't have much, other than some lines about lighting farts. Just kidding.

My dad walked into the room, reading a newspaper. "Morning, boys."

"Hey, Dad," I said through a mouthful of Raisin Bran.

Derek looked up from his show and asked, "What's that?"

"What are you talking about?" Dad asked. "This? It's a newspaper?"

"Oh," Derek said.

What an idiot. Kids today, man, I'm tellin' ya.

"I heard there's something interesting in here," my dad said, looking at me.

"What?"

He opened to the entertainment section and showed me. "An article highlighting the band's entrance to the Battle of the Bands contest as a mysterious and up-and-coming new entrant."

"Big deal," Derek said.

"It is a big deal," my dad said.

"If it's not Derek in the spotlight, he doesn't care," I said. My brother was the best at mainly everything. He didn't like it during the 1% of the time I was good at something.

"I'm disappointed, Derek." My dad looked at me and said, "Let's forget about that for a minute. Here's the article, 'Mayhem? Mad Men? You might think putting the two together would be a bad idea. You would be wrong. Mayhem Mad Men is a talented, up-and-coming new band. While not expected to win Battle of the Bands later this summer, this writer expects them to win some fans along the way.' Nice article."

"Thanks, Dad," I said, while Derek stewed.

ON THE BUS heading to camp, Derek made an uncharacteristic trip from the back row of the bus (where the cool kids sat) up to front (where Nerd Nation laid claim) to be an annoying jerk. What else is new?

"Hey, guys," Derek said, enthusiastically.

"What do you want?" I asked, skeptical. He either wanted something or was pretending to be nice to lure us into some sort of trap.

"I want to join the band," he said to the rest of the band, except for Sly, who took a different bus or got dropped off or maybe rode his own motorcycle. Nobody knew for sure.

"What instrument do you play?" Just Charles asked, his brow furrowed.

"Lead singer," Derek said, simply.

"I'm the lead singer, idiot," I said, pointedly.

"Not anymore," Derek said with a smirk. "Right, guys? With me as the front man, do you know how many girls will go crazy for you all?"

"Get out of here, Derek. You've never sung a tune in your life. And the whole band hates you."

Just Charles smiled and said, "I don't."

"Stop sucking up," I said to Just Charles and then to Derek, "He's just afraid of you. This is so typical. As soon as the spotlight is on me, you try to steal it from me. Go back to your seat with the rest of the bullies and future criminals."

My brother was such an idiot. My parents are smart, decent people. I don't know how they messed up so badly. I was so annoyed that when we arrived, I headed straight for Max's. I needed a break. I hoped he had some sort of massage therapy or counseling services in place.

"Why do you always kiss up to him?" I asked Just Charles.

"Isn't it obvious? I don't want him to beat me up."

I looked down at his feet. There was an oversized duffle bag. "What's in the bag?"

"A new look for the ladies," he said, smiling.

Oh, God. I hoped he wouldn't embarrass himself too much. I was wrong.

WALKING in to Max's was like an oasis. I don't know why I got surprised each time, but it was always so crazy. There was a water feature in the corner, consisting of rocks and a waterfall. Two people lay face down on massage tables, getting massages from people I had never seen before.

I pumped my fist. "Yes!"

"Shhh," Max said. "Try to keep the excitement level down. This is a spa, not a sporting event." He placed a Hawaiian lei over my head and handed me a frozen drink with an umbrella in it.

"Sorry. I could really use a massage right now," I said. Plus, I was glad that Max finally hadn't caught me by surprise with his product offering.

"The life of a musician can be a tough one," he said.

"Don't I know it," I said. "What's that smell?" I asked.

"That's the pig roasting."

I just shook my head with a chuckle. Max was unbelievable.

"I can fit you in Tuesday at four? Does that work? We're jammed up for a while."

"How are you booked up for two days? Who are these people?"

"I'm sorry, but our clientele demands absolute anonymity."

"Of course. I'll figure something out."

"Come back for the luau at two, okay?" Max said. "Mahalo!"

I nodded my head, dumbfounded.

My dumbfoundedness continued when I walked outside to meet the rest of the band and camp group. I saw Just Charles and kind of forgot it was summer and eighty degrees. He wore a floor-length fur coat with a puffy collar and oversized sun glasses.

I looked around wondering if I was on a hidden camera TV show or something.

I walked up to the group of Ben, Luke, Just Charles, and Sly, and asked Just Charles, "Is that a real fur coat?"

"Of course not, but it looks legit right?"

"I'm totally getting one, too," Luke said. "Or six."

"Dude, it's the middle of the summer. What the heck are you doing? And where did you even get that?"

"Did you read that article in the paper? We're like superstars. We gotta dress the part."

"What part is that?" Ben asked. "You look like a giant otter or something."

"That's hurtful. I like this. I found it in the closet. I think it was my Grandmother's."

Sly laughed and said, "Yeah, real legit rock star in our presence."

We all laughed, except for Just Charles.

I heard laughter behind us and saw Sammie, Sophie, and Ditzy Dayna walking over, admiring Just Charles' new wardrobe choice.

"Nice. I like it," Dayna said.

"Isn't that a little hot, Charles?" Sophie asked.

"Yes. Ridiculously hot. I might jump in the pool with this thing on."

"A rock star would totally do that," Luke said. I wasn't sure if he was kidding and trying to get Just Charles to cannonball into the pool with a fur coat on or if he was really serious.

Brody whistled behind us. He was kind of on time. My sister probably made it clear that she was not interested. I hoped he was finally giving up.

"We gotta go," I said to Sophie. "See you later."

"Later," she said.

I turned to leave and started walking with the rest of the crew. I glanced to my side and Sly wasn't there. I turned back around and saw him talking to Sophie.

Sly said, "I want to play a song for you."

"Okay," she said, cautiously.

"Hey, Sly. Let's go," I said.

Sly turned and headed my way. Sophie looked at me and shrugged.

"What was that about?" I asked.

"Nothin'. Just talking music," Sly said, walking ahead of me.

I was starting to get annoyed with Luke and Sly. Sophie was my girlfriend, not the band's. It was driving me crazy. I had to stop thinking about it or I knew I would go crazy and do something stupid and get myself in trouble with Sophie. I mean, none of it was her fault. You can't blame her for being nearly perfect. She had once dated Randy Warblemacher for a short time period, so I knew she wasn't totally perfect, but she was as close as they come.

I decided to throw myself into the music to get my mind off things. Everyone loved our new song, "Middle School Mayhem". I wanted to write another one. True, I hadn't written the first one on my own. We had a songwriting sleepover to thank for that, but I was going to try anyway.

It did not start off great. I sat in the den with my iPad, just staring at a flashing cursor. For like an hour. I remembered the inspiration for our first song. Writing about what we knew. About our lives. I listed all the strange and horrible things about middle school- the food, gym class, the smell of most kids after gym class, idiot principals. I thought about our hopes, our dreams, our fears. I didn't know what to write about until I started to get hungry and then it hit me. That strange feeling when you know you're hungry, so hungry, but you also know that the only way to satisfy that hunger is to eat in the school cafeteria, where we put our lives in danger every day.

And then the floodgates opened up. I just started singing, "It's the middle of the school day and you're feeling kinda hungraaaay, so you head down to the cafeteria with a little bit of fear in ya. Cafeteria delirium!"

I kept writing verse after verse, crushing it. I was half concerned that the Cherry Avenue middle school cafeteria staff would be upset with me, but it's not like they could make the food any worse in retaliation.

Plus, I was probably going to be home schooled as we set out on tour! With another hit, we were going to be rock stars!

～

OUR METEORIC RISE to superstardom was not without its setbacks. We had another birthday party gig. We were moving up the maturity chart. This one was for an eight-year-old girl. I tried some new moves that Leighton and Sophie had taught me and watched a lot of YouTube videos. Perhaps, I was a little too confident. I nearly knocked myself out with the microphone pole. For a minute, I thought I had broken my nose. It's sad, but people thought me writhing in pain was dancing.

The good news was that it got us another show. After the party, the six of us were hanging at Frank's pizza when Brody got a call.

"Mad Men hotline," he said, coolly. He waited for a moment listening to the person on the other end. "Well, our schedule is really tight. I'm not sure we can fit you in. Let me check our calendar." He waited for a minute and checked no calendars. "You're in luck. We're free that weekend. Yes, a thousand dollars for the set. Nonnegotiable...Okay, nine hundred...Seven fifty, it is. Talk soon. Ciao."

Brody looked at us and said, "Good news," and then whispered, "and a little bad."

"What is it?" I asked.

"We just booked the County Fair for $750."

"What's bad about that?" Ben asked. "That's awesome!"

"Well, we're opening for another band."

"So," Sly said.

"That band is, umm, Love Puddle."

"No way," I said. "I'm not doing it. That's Randy's stupid band."

Brody backtracked. "Did I say opening? I meant that due to scheduling constraints, we are just performing before them."

"You expect us to believe that?" Just Charles asked.

"I was hoping, yes," Brody said.

The band all looked at me. Luke said, "We gotta do it.

Come on, Aus. This is big. Just Charles can buy a real fur coat after this one."

Being the math whiz that I was, I calculated Just Charles' cut and realized that was not even close to being accurate, but I didn't want to be the prissy lead singer and kill the mood.

I took a deep breath. "If you guys want to do it, I'll suck it up and do it."

The group cheered and clinked pizza slices. I was just glad we didn't try a high-five.

But by the next day, I was having second thoughts. I approached Brody privately at camp and said, "Hey, I'm not really feeling this new gig. Can you try to get us something as good?"

"No way, man. The press is all over this. Plus, I got pyrotechnics."

"Pyro what nits?" I asked.

"You know, like fireworks."

"Oh, we gotta have that."

"Good, I'm glad you agree. I already got the Fire Marshal's approval. And my brother broke the law in like six states just to get them here."

The band came over, wondering what was going on.

I knew that because Sly came over and said, "Hey, what's going on?"

"Nothing. Just talking music," I said, remembering his response to me when he was cozying up to Sophie.

"I'll play the County Fair if we all agree to get Randy good."

"Done," Ben said. The rest of the band nodded.

"Nice. I think I have an idea." I looked at Just Charles. "What kind of keyboard does Love Puddle use?"

"The same as mine. Why?"

"It hooks up to a laptop, right?"

"Yep."

"I think we should make some adjustments to theirs before the County Fair."

"Like what?" Luke asked.

"Do you remember Principal Buthaire's computer malfunction?"

Smiles broke out among my band mates. It was going to be epic. If you've never heard the computer story, just hang on. You'll get the gist soon enough.

17

It was the morning of the county fair. Even though I knew Randy and Love Puddle would be there, I was hoping not to bump into them. We were set for the run through with the stage manager a few hours before our set. But then Mr. Smarty Pants thought it would be a great idea to save himself time and schedule both bands for a run through at the same time.

We walked up to see Love Puddle in a huddle. I was not feeling any of their so-called love. I think it was all a sham. We kept to ourselves as we waited for the stage manager to arrive, but of course, Randy couldn't help himself. He strolled over with his typical smirk on his face, like he knew something we didn't.

"Hey Davenfart," he called, "I didn't think you had the guts to open for Love Puddle. Respect."

"Get over yourself, Randolph. We're not opening for you. You're entertaining the leftovers from our show."

"Oh, really?" Randy asked, laughing. "You don't have the moves to make that true, Davenfart." Randy proceeded to bust out some crazy dance stuff that you would see in a real music video.

"I got the moves," I said, without showing anyone my moves.

"Show me," Randy said, eyebrows raised.

"No," I said.

"'Cause you don't have 'em."

"No, I just don't want to. I'm not gonna waste my talents on your stupid face."

"That's enough, boys," The stage manager called out. He looked at Love Puddle and said, "Why don't you come back after the first act and we'll finish it up."

Randy looked at me and said, "First act. That's the opening act."

"Shut your dumb face," I said, shaking my head as he walked away, laughing.

AFTER THE SOUND check and a quick break, the crowd started to gather as we waited on the side of the stage. There had to be a hundred people there and it was still a few minutes before show time. Once we started playing, more people would come. Unless we were terrible and they ran away from the noise, which was entirely possible.

Mr. Muscalini had arrived to support us. He had kind of become our mascot/motivational speaker, although he wasn't always motivating.

Brody took a deep breath and said, "I hope this goes well."

Mr. Muscalini chimed in and added, "Or really badly in an embarrassing and fun way."

See what I mean? "Fun for who?" I asked, angrily.

Mr. Muscalini responded, "The rest of us. Now, get out there and entertain us!" He looked at Brody and said, "After this, we have to go support your mother in the contest."

"What contest?" Ben asked.

"She's in the pie-eating contest. She's won it eleven years in a row," Brody said.

"That's...awesome," I said. "I'm sure you're really proud."

"Nah, it kinda stinks, man. I can only eat one slice of pie before the sugar gets to me. She's very disappointed in me."

"I wish my mother wanted me to eat more pie," Just Charles said, disappointed.

And then the stage manager called out, "You're on, Mayhem Mad Men!"

We hustled out on stage and got set up. I walked over to Ben with a pair of glaucoma shades in my hand that my dad got me at the pharmacy. He had the bandana and the head-phones ready.

As I stood in front of Ben, I said, "I got this idea at the old age home. Now, with the pyrotechnics, it makes even more sense."

"Pyro whatzitz?" Ben asked, nervously.

"Pretend I didn't say anything. Just know you're gonna look so cool."

I put the bandana on Ben's head, followed by the over-sized shades and then the headphones.

"Wait thirty seconds and then go," I said.

"What?" Ben screamed. And then, "One, two, three!"

I rushed back to the front of the stage and grabbed the mic as the crew started playing. I saw my parents, sister, Sophie, and Sammie out in the crowd. I didn't have time to wave.

I started to sing our hit, "6 A.M. wakeup. The halls are filled with too much body spray, perfume and makeup. I gotta claw through the fumes just to get to the bathroom."

The crowd was going wild. I was feeling it. More than I'd ever felt it before. The crowd's energy surged through my body like a lightning bolt. I grabbed the microphone pole and started strumming it like a guitar as Sly let it rip on his own guitar. I think I may have even closed my eyes while I played the air guitar. You don't have to say it. I know. It was bad.

The roar of the crowd seemed to get us all going. I ran across the stage singing as I went. Luke threw his bass in the air. The crowd gasped. He wobbled underneath it, trying to line it up for the catch. As you know, we were not the most athletic bunch. I was afraid it might smash Luke in the face and end the show right then and there. But he caught it! And kept playing without missing a beat.

Then the pyrotechnics hit. Eight Sparkulars exploded simultaneously, sending streams of sparks into the air around the stage. The crowd's energy rose even further. We were crushing it. Love Puddle was going down. There was no way they could best us after that. And they didn't even have a pool that time.

I looked out into the crowd. It was at least ten people deep across the entire stage. People were jumping with their hands up. I heard a few people yell, "Jump!"

I remembered the crowd surfing that Cameron Quinn of Goat Turd did at Camp Cherriwacka and how awesome it was. And then my sister's words echoed in my mind, "You're not a singer. You're an entertainer." I decided to give them some entertainment. Like a boss, Aus.

For some reason, I held my breath before I jumped. I

took a step back and then hopped into the crowd. The whole crowd scattered faster than seemed humanly possible or I somehow was flying in slow motion. Only one lady didn't seem to know that she was supposed to get the heck out of there or she was the only one brave enough to stick around to try and catch me. I actually think I remembered her from Vintage Retirement Community. She was old and apparently very slow, and I was headed straight for her like a WWE wrestler jumping off the top rope for a body slam.

I closed my eyes, somehow thinking that might help ease the blow, but we collided with massive force, our heads connecting with a serious smash. Our lips may have actually met for a brief second. I'm guessing because I don't actually remember. I mean, that's the only way I could've ended up with her dentures in my mouth, but I don't want to talk about that.

When I woke up, there was a crowd around me. Or some strange ritual occurred while I was unconscious where everyone left their empty shoes around me in a circle. I turned to my side and spit out the old lady's teeth.

My mother shrieked, "Oh, my God! He lost all of his teeth!"

My dad said, "I'm pretty sure he had braces."

Ben took a closer look at the teeth and said, "I think those are the old lady's."

There were a few hurling sounds from the crowd as I sat up. It would've been nice if people expressed their happiness that I was okay, but after getting a look at the dentures, I kind of didn't blame them.

My father offered me a hand and helped me up. I looked past him to see Randy and Regan pointing and laughing. Ugh. I closed my eyes, hoping I would return to unconsciousness again. But then I remembered what we had planned for their performance. They were in for a rude awakening.

The Mad Men regrouped behind the stage. The excitement level was off the charts. Nobody had ever seen a middle school kid spit out someone else's dentures. Oh, and despite the disastrous and abrupt end to our performance, apparently, it didn't dampen the crowd's love of the performance. Perhaps our dorkiness was even part of our charm. After all, we were middle school kids singing about dumb stuff that happens at middle school.

The crew was thinking big. Luke said, "Should we record an album or a demo or something?"

Just Charles said, "I think we're ready to go on tour. Who should open for us?"

Mr. Muscalini stepped forward and said, "This was a big win. I mean Gordo looks like a wacko out there on the drums, but guess what? Most drummers are wackos. And there was a little mishap with Davenport there on the crowd surfing...you'll get the hang of it. Just glad nobody was hurt."

Ben chimed in, "Well, there was the old lady."

Just Charles added, "We really should visit her in the hospital. The EMTs said it wasn't good."

Sophie and Sammie ran around the corner to us.

Sophie said to me, "You sure you're okay?"

"Yep."

"You're not going to start speaking in gibberish like you did during the Santukkah! musical?"

"Negatory," I said.

"Good." She looked at Luke and said, "You played a fab bass! It was awesome."

Luke's face nearly exploded into a smile. "Thanks! You really think so? I mean, it felt good. You really inspired me to be better."

Sophie looked at me and asked, "What's wrong?"

"Nothing," I said. I didn't really know. Sophie didn't do anything wrong by helping Luke, but I didn't like wondering whether or not Luke, and Sly, for that matter, liked her, too.

Before we got into it, Brody came over to us, giddy. "It's time. The sound check is done and they don't go on for ten minutes. It's now or never."

Just Charles and I looked at each other.

"You ready?" I asked.

"No, but let's go. I'll get the laptop. You're plugging it in."

"You said you would! I don't know where the cable goes."

"It's a cable. You plug it in," Just Charles said, annoyed.

"Still, you're doing it," I said. Really mature, I know.

Just Charles mocked me as he grabbed the laptop. "Still, you're doing it. I'm Austin Davenport. I can't plug in a cable."

"Fine, I'll do it," I said.

"Good luck," Ben said.

Luke saluted me and I got a few nods from the others.

I peeked around the side of the stage with Just Charles on my heels. I saw a crowd in the distance, but nobody from

Love Puddle or any official-looking people. I rushed toward the front of the stage and stopped midway. I heard voices in front of it. I hoped nobody was up on the stage.

I ducked my head under the curtain, saw the keyboard, and that the stage was empty.

"Okay, boost me up," I said to Just Charles.

"You didn't say anything about boosting," Just Charles said, fumbling with the laptop.

"Then I'll boost you and you plug it in."

"Again, with the plugging," Just Charles said, placing the laptop down. "I'll boost you. I need to do the download."

"Good point," I said.

We weren't the boosting type. Climbing stuff usually leads to falling, which leads to embarrassment in front of peers, so nerds typically avoid it. But if we wanted to stick it to Randy and Love Puddle, we were going to have to give it a shot.

"How do I do this?" Just Charles asked, taking an enormously wide stance.

"What are you doing?" I asked, looking around. No one seemed to notice us.

"Just climb on," he said, interlocking his fingers and bending down, offering me a step.

I ducked under the curtain, put my hands on the stage, and said, "Let 'er rip."

Just Charles grunted and lifted me. About an inch. I stood up on his hand and pushed. I felt his hand hit the ground.

"Oww, you crushed my fingers," Just Charles whisper-yelled at me.

"You should've done the plugging," I said, annoyed. "Get down. I'll stand on your back."

"You're not standing on my back."

"I am if you want to win...and keep all of your fingers."

"Fine," Just Charles said, getting down on his hands and knees.

I stepped up onto his back. He grunted again. I could feel him shaking. I tried to balance on his back as I tussled with the curtain. After a minute of fumbling, I was underneath it and got my upper body on the stage. I kicked my feet as I slithered forward onto the stage. My foot connected with something hard. I kept going and finally made it up onto the stage, beneath the keyboard.

I spun around on my stomach, my feet nearly taking out said keyboard, and causing it to skid across the floor and almost tip over. Despite my nerd-like reflexes, I was able to grab the keyboard before it hit the ground. I put it back in place and carefully peeked out from under the curtain, waiting for Just Charles to hand me the cable.

My heart leapt. Just Charles lay on the ground, holding his nose.

"You kicked me in the face," he said, angrily. "I know, I should've plugged in the cable."

"No time to discuss. Hand it to me, now."

"Why are you in such a hurry?"

"Duh, we're hacking their keyboard," I said. I mean, honestly. And he's supposed to be smarter than the others.

I grabbed the cable from Just Charles' outstretched hand and turned back around. I plugged it in from underneath the keyboard. And then I heard voices and footsteps.

It was Randy. I could pick out his arrogant walk anywhere. Or maybe it was because I heard Nick DeRozan say in his manly voice, "Come on, Warblemacher. We gotta get set."

I panicked. The beast of a middle schooler that was Nick DeRozan was coming my way, his drums set right behind the keyboard, and more importantly, me. I rolled to the side. There was no way I was going to let Nick see me there. He might stuff me in a drum, never to be found again. I'd have to endure the constant pummeling of his meaty hands for all eternity.

"Hey!" I heard Nick say.

I didn't have a chance to get situated properly so I just rolled myself off the stage, splattering to the ground, puked out by the curtain. The cable came with me. I hoped it was done uploading our attack. Because we were going to be done if we stuck around any longer. I just hoped Nick hadn't recognized me.

"Let's go," I said, scrambling to my feet and pulling Just Charles behind me. The cable dragged in the dirt as he ran with the laptop. I hoped Nick wasn't smart enough to follow our trail.

Just Charles and I rushed back to the band.

"How'd it go?" Brody asked.

"Give me your bandana and glasses," I said to Ben.

"That good, huh?" Brody asked.

I put the glasses on as quickly as I could and tied the bandana around my head like a do rag. I felt like an elderly biker, if there is such a thing.

"Let's get out of here," I said.

Brody ushered us into the growing crowd. I peeked into the stage from the front and saw Love Puddle fully assembled. Even Nick DeRozan was there and sitting on his stool in front of the drums.

"Now what?" Sly asked.

"Now we watch them go up in smoke," Ben said.

"Actually, more like a fart cloud," I corrected. "If it worked. We pulled the plug when Nick came up on stage."

"I guess we'll have to see," Brody said.

And then we heard Love Puddle's manager yell into the microphone, "Are you ready for it to rain love?" The crowd screamed. "I give you Love Puddle!"

"Can't wait to see it rain love, whatever that means," I said, laughing.

The rest of Mayhem Mad Men and I watched Love Puddle from the back of the crowd. Randy walked out to the middle of the stage and smiled at the screaming crowd. He held the microphone to his mouth, and yelled, "Hit it!"

Nick DeRozan led off with a mini-drum solo and then a guitar joined in. It sounded pretty good to start, but we were waiting for the keyboardist. Randy was swinging the microphone stand around, waiting to sing, while nodding his head rhythmically to the music.

And then the moment we had been waiting for kicked in. The keyboardist started pounding on the keys. And it was glorious.

With each press of a key, a fart reverberated throughout the crowd, echoing from the speakers. They were almost melodic. It was like someone was farting in tune with the rest of the band. And that's because he was. Laughter erupted from the crowd. Everyone was wondering what the heck is going on.

Randy's face flushed red, standing up on the stage in front of everyone, not sure of what to do. He yelled over to the keyboardist, "It's you, idiot! Stop playing!" And then he ran over to the keyboardist who continued to rock the stage with supersonic farts. The keyboardist looked up at Randy, confused.

Randy pulled the cord out of the outlet and all the music fizzled to a stop.

The keyboardist's voice echoed through the speakers, "What's your problem, man?"

"You're stinking up the place," Randy said, walking away.

The crowd continued to laugh and chatter about the craziness that had just happened.

"I thought it sounded good," he said, to more laughter.

"That was awesome!" Sly said. "high-five?"

The rest of us just shook our heads and mumbled. Sly was disappointed.

Love Puddle's manager hurried to the stage and ducked, as Randy's microphone hurtled through the air on target for a direct hit to his face. I guess Randy was a tad annoyed.

The manager dodged the blow, steadied himself, and addressed the crowd without the microphone. "We're having some technical difficulties. Please stand by."

I couldn't hear what was being said after that because Randy had chucked the microphone, being the typical mature kid that he was, but they were flustered and animated as they tried to figure out what the heck had happened, and more importantly, how to fix it.

After a few minutes, the manager returned to the front of the stage with the mic in hand and said, "Okay, we're going to try this again." He handed the microphone to Randy and hurried off the stage before Randy could get angry and rifle it at him again.

We continued to watch as Love Puddle bounced back from the disaster. Randy worked the crowd, shaking hands, giving high-fives (unfortunately without falling), and singing to girls at the front of the stage. Regan did not look happy.

All in all, it was a great day at the County Fair. Well, except for the local media's portrayal of it. Which, of course you know by now, Derek was on top of like it was the story of the year. I mean, did he use some sort of alert system to figure out every time I got caught embarrassing myself on camera?

I SAT in the den with my parents, reading while they messed around on their iPads. You know parents and their devices. Anyway, Derek rushed in, screaming about the band being on the news. He grabbed the remote, turned on the TV, and flipped the channel to our local news station.

Calvin Conklin, a pompous newscaster who once thought I was a time traveler when he interviewed me at our science fair, stood in front of the stage at the County Fair.

"Calvin Conklin here at the County Fair where two up-and-coming bands, well one perhaps falling, pun intended, performed for the crowd."

Calvin smiled like a jerk and then the camera cut to footage from our concert. I was on stage as the Sparkulars exploded into the air and then I proceeded to flatten an old lady. Well, you know the rest.

Derek laughed uncontrollably. I had pretty much come to expect his lack of support.

"Enough, Derek," my father said.

"It's okay. He can keep laughing. Love Puddle's keyboardist is about to stink up the stage. Here it is," I said, pointing.

The footage cut to Randy singing his second song, slapping hands and winking at girls.

Calvin's voice accompanied the footage, "Love Puddle rocked the County Fair today with front man Randy Warblemacher entertaining the crowd on a fabulous summer day."

The camera cut back to Calvin. His excessively white

smile lit up the screen. He said, "Young Warblemacher is a handsome boy. Kind of reminds me of myself back in the day. And today. Back to you, Ted."

"How could they not show the farting keyboard?"

"I guess you embarrassed Rock 'n Roll enough for one day," Derek said.

18

We met up at Brody's house the next day to regroup and get some practice in. The band, plus Mr. Muscalini, stood in a wide semicircle as Brody spoke to us.

"Gentlemen," Brody said, looking at us.

"Who is he talking to?" Ben asked me, looking around.

Even Mr. Muscalini was curious as to who Brody was talking to.

Brody looked at us, "You, all of you, pay attention. Despite Aus crushing an old lady, who remains in critical condition, we'll have to send her some flowers or something, Calvin Conklin's excerpt on our band got the attention of some very important people in the music biz."

"Katy Perry?" Luke asked.

"Taylor Swift?" Just Charles asked.

"No," Brody said.

"Oooh, oooh, that guy from America's Got Talent with the funny accent?" Mr. Muscalini asked.

Brody took a deep breath and exhaled, frustrated.

"No, the talent manager at The Sound! They can hold like a thousand people and they want the Mad Men!"

We all let out cheers. Mr. Muscalini threw out a monster fist pump, the force so strong, the wind from it almost knocked all our skinny bodies over.

"We need to do something fresh," I said.

"A new song," Sly said.

"Songwriting sleepover?" Ben asked.

"It worked for us once," I said. "Who's in?"

Mr. Muscalini yelled, "You know I'm in!"

I looked around at the rest of the band and then back at Mr. Muscalini. "I don't know if my parents will think that's such a good idea."

Mr. Muscalini nodded with a sad frown on his face.

I looked at Sly and said, "You in this time?"

He shook his head and said, "Nah, don't want to mess with what worked last time."

WE STAYED up half the night trying to recreate the magic from our last songwriting sleepover that gave us "Middle School Mayhem". It wasn't working. Just Charles was on his fifth soda and was talking so fast, we could barely understand what he was saying and Luke had so much pizza he had passed out on the couch. It was really just me and Ben grappling with a new song idea.

Just Charles paced around the room and said, "Birdy tld us ta write whatweno."

Austin said, "What are you saying?"

"Write whatweno!" Just Charles said, angrily.

"That's Just Charles' evil alter ego, Chugging Chuck," Ben said, laughing.

"Write it down," I told Just Charles.

He grabbed a piece of paper and scribbled, "Brody told us to write what we know!!!!!" and then underlined it a lot.

"Oh, right," I said.

"Ya geyser 'sposedtabethesmartones," Just Charles said.

"Dude, I think you need to eat some vegetables or something to counteract the soda."

Just Charles sat down and threw the pen across the room, frustrated.

"Write what we know," Ben said.

"Doweave any hatersyet?" Just Charles asked.

"Haters? I don't think so. Well, not because we're too good, anyway. But what do we hate?" I asked.

"We already blasted cafeteria food. I kinda hate gym," Ben said.

"Me, too. But Mr. Muscalini would be mad if we blasted gym class."

"It could just be about how we stink at gym even though we want to be good."

"I thinkalikedat!" Just Charles said, smiling.

"He likes it!" Ben said.

"Nice. Okay. Let me think for a minute," I said, standing up. "Trying to be a star...and make coach proud."

"But when the QB yells hike," Ben added, "I fall straight to the ground."

Just Charles was so excited, he jumped up and down, not even able to speak.

I sang out the next line, "Breathing's getting heavy, so I call time out and pretend to tie my laces."

"Duck behind my classmates to..."

"avoid a dodgeball to my face, man!" I yelled. "Tryin' to be a sports star hero, but a nerd like me will never be more than a gym class zero."

"You a hero?" Ben asked.

"Nah, man, I'm a gym class zero." I did a celebratory dance, nearly knocking over a few pictures on a nearby shelf.

Just Charles yelled out, "Boommicdrop."

"Boom. Mic drop is right," Ben said. "Holy cow! I'm bilingual! I can speak Evil Chuck!"

WE WERE backstage at The Sound. Like always, we were one inch away from peeing in our pants, we were so nervous. I didn't dare look out at the crowd. I didn't want Ben to look. His bladder would explode. Even without looking, we knew it was a big crowd because we could hear the buzz of hundreds of voices talking.

Brody walked up to us and, of course, said the wrong thing. "I can't believe how many people are here! This is gonna be awesome! You guys nervous? I mean, I would be with that many people out there."

Ben's face was ghost white and seemingly made of stone. His eyes weren't even blinking.

"Who are we opening for?" Sly asked.

"You're the headliner," Brody answered. "Small Noggin is opening for you."

"Really? That's crazy," I said. It was kind of exciting and kind of pee-in-your-pants scary.

Just Charles and Luke were stunned. Ben actually looked kinda better because his stomach was convulsing, likely ready to puke, but I thought that was a positive, because his body was working again.

Brody said, "Oh, and other great news! My brother just got back from Mexico with a truckload of pyrotechnics.

We're gonna light up the night sky like the 4th of July." He looked at us, eyes wide. "Dudes, that should be a song."

Just Charles said, "Our creative department will take it into consideration..."

"One little problem," I said. "We're indoors and there's a ceiling. How big can the fireworks be?"

"Oh, I hadn't thought of that." Brody shrugged. "We'll just let it fly."

"Sounds good to us," Luke said.

Ben chimed in, holding up the glaucoma shades, "Umm, these shades are great, well, not looking, but they keep the light out. I hope I don't find it too distracting if the pyrotechnics get crazy."

"You'll be fine. Don't worry about," I said.

"I'd feel better without them," Ben said.

"So, lose the glasses," Brody said.

"I meant the pyrotechnics," Ben answered.

Brody looked like he was gonna cry.

"Always draggin' us down," Sly said under his breath.

"What'd you say?" Ben asked, angrily. He stepped forward toward Sly. "I'm getting tired of you trashing me all the time."

"Well, maybe you shouldn't play like trash then."

"Enough," Brody said, stepping in between them. "The pyrotechnics make the show."

"I guess the rest of us don't matter," Luke said.

"I didn't mean it-" Brody was distracted, looking out at the stage. "You guys, it's your time! Get out there!"

I STOOD out on the center of the stage, looking out at the

crowd. It was packed. There wasn't an empty seat in the place. I swallowed hard, took a deep breath, and said, "We've got a brand-new song that we wrote specifically for all of you here at The Sound," I said. "It's called, "Gym Class Zero.""

Ben clicked his sticks together and kicked us off. Luke and Just Charles followed with Sly right behind. I looked out into the huge crowd, glad I had just tinkled before I went out onto the stage, and started singing.

"Trying to be a star and make coach proud. But when the QB yells hike, I fall straight to the ground."

The crowd's energy took off like a rocket and that was before the pyrotechnics kicked it. Brody pressed the button to ignite them. There were so many Sparkulars that the stage lit up so bright, I couldn't even see the crowd in front of me. I knew enough to stop walking around. I didn't want to fall off the stage again.

The crowd loved it. People were jumping up and down all over the place and well, creating mayhem.

We were heading toward our finale, so I headed over to Just Charles. Luke met me there, bass in hand. I held out the microphone for the two of them to join in.

We finished off the song with Just Charles and Luke shouting into the mic together, "You a hero?"

I said, "Nah, man. I'm a gym class zero."

More Sparkulars went off and then the crowd went wild. People were screaming, whistling, and a few people even rushed the stage. Security promptly flattened them like pancakes, but still it was cool that we had people who wanted to come up on the stage. We had graduated to the next level. It felt awesome to hear them cheering our little band of five middle schoolers who sing about dumb stuff and middle school.

When we came off the stage, Mr. Muscalini was waiting for us.

"That...was...beautiful," Mr. Muscalini said, wiping his eyes. "All I care about is that you try. You don't have to be able to dunk like me. I don't expect that. I mean, look at my calves for God's sake. They're like bigger than those stupid smart cars." He looked at us, confused. "Where was I?"

"You just care that we try?" I asked.

Mr. Muscalini started to tear up again. "There are no zeroes here. Only heroes. Bring it in."

We all took a step forward and got ready for a high-five.

"Uh, uh. We hug it out on this one."

Mr. Muscalini engulfed us with his giant arms and hands and squeezed.

Our heads all clunked together. "Oww!" I wasn't sure what would happen first: would my head pop off or my ribs implode?

"I love you no matter what," Mr. Muscalini said.

"Does it get this weird at school?" Sly grunted.

"Pretty much," I said, nodding.

I COULDN'T WAIT to call Sophie and tell her about our gig. I picked up the phone and dialed.

"Hey, Austin," Sophie said.

"Hey," I said. "How are you?"

"Good. Doing a video practice with Luke on my iPad. Can I call you back? He told me how great the concert was. I'm so happy for you guys."

The energy drained from my body. "Yeah, it went great," I said, disappointed.

"Doesn't sound like it," she said. "What's wrong?"

"Nothing. I guess call me when you're done with Luke."

I hung up before she even acknowledged it. I kinda felt bad because she didn't do anything wrong. She was just helping him, but I was just so annoyed, I couldn't help it.

And then it got worse. We all reported to Brody's for practice the next day. Well, all of us except for Luke.

Even Just Charles was annoyed, which was saying something. "Will somebody call him? I'm so tired of this," Just Charles said.

"I'm not doing it," I said.

"Fine," Ben said, taking out his phone.

Ben pressed Luke's name in his phone's favorites and dialed. "Where are you?" he asked. "Well, are you coming?" Ben paused for a minute and then said, annoyed, "What do you mean you'll have your people talk to my people? We are your people...Well, then who are my people? ugh. Just get over here. Everybody's mad. You'll see?" Ben hung up the phone with disgust.

Ben looked at the rest of us and said, "I don't know if he's coming." He looked at Brody and said, "Can we talk about dropping the pyrotechnics? They're very distracting."

"No way!" Brody said. "The people love them."

"Maybe we can add a rap instead," I said. I liked the pyrotechnics, but I wanted to make sure Ben knew I supported him. "I did a mean rap in our musical, Santukkah! I gotta Maccabee Me!" I rapped my Hanukkah rap about Judah Maccabee.

"That's sweet," Sly said, less than enthused. "But I think that's a bad idea. Brody's right." He looked at Ben. "Nobody else has a problem with them."

"Whatever," Ben said, annoyed.

Before it turned into an argument, a car pulled up, and

Luke hopped out with his equipment. We all just stared at him as he walked up toward the garage.

"You're late, dude," Brody said.

Luke scoffed, "What? We're a band. Nobody shows up on time when you're a rock star."

"You're gonna find yourself out of the band if you don't make it to practice."

I looked at Luke and said, "Yeah, even Randy and Derek show up to practice with Mr. Muscalini."

"Whatever."

"It's funny that you don't want to practice with us, but you seem just fine practicing with Sophie," I said.

He ignored me and looked at Just Charles and asked, "When's our video hitting YouTube?"

Just Charles frowned. "We never did a video."

"What? Why not?"

I kept pressing. I was still annoyed. "You seem to be practicing a lot with my girlfriend. We didn't have enough time for that video."

Luke stuttered, "Yeah, well, I just need to get better at playing the bass, not practicing the songs. It's different."

"Yeah, the only thing that's different is that she's not in the band, so you don't get to practice with her."

"What are you trying to say?" Luke said, angrily.

"I'm not trying to say anything. I said it."

Luke gritted his teeth and said, "Remind me what you said?"

I thought for a moment and scratched my head. "I forgot. I think you like my girlfriend."

"What? No. Dude," Luke said.

I pointed to Luke's hands. "Your fingers were crossed."

"No, they weren't," Luke said, defensively.

"You know that doesn't really do anything, right?" Ben said.

Brody's face dropped, "Really? Ahh, that stinks."

And then Sammie came running over like she just won the lottery or something. Her smile stretched ear to ear.

I looked at her and asked, "What's going on? Why are you so happy?"

"Randy got dumped by Regan!"

"That's cold, Sammie," Ben said.

"Well, I feel bad for him, but I'm happy because well, you know."

"She likes Randy in case you haven't noticed," Luke said to Sly, who had no idea what was going on.

I was still mad about Luke lying to me to enjoy Randy's misery.

"Can you go with me to see Love Puddle's next performance?"

"Sure," I said, totally not wanting to. Not unless the keyboard started farting again and I was pretty convinced they wouldn't let that happen again.

19

I stood in my dining room where the entire wall was covered with mirrors. My brother was engulfed with PlayStation, so I had a few minutes of harassment-free time to try to practice my dance moves. I stood in front of the mirror and felt like an idiot.

I was surprised by footsteps, so I stopped and pretended to check out a smudge on the mirror.

"Don't worry, it's just me," Leighton said. "How are the moves coming?"

"They're okay."

"Are you practicing?"

"Trying. It's hard to look at myself dancing in the mirror."

"Why don't you video tape it?"

"That's worse. Plus, if Derek ever got a hold of it, the whole world would know how bad I am."

"What moves are you doing? Show me."

"I still kinda don't have any," I scratched my head, thinking.

"I have an idea. You might not like it, but I think it'll be good. When's Love Puddle's next performance?"

"This afternoon. Mom is taking Sammie, Sophie, and me."

"And me, too," Leighton said.

"You're coming?"

"Yeah. You need to learn some moves from Randy."

"I don't want to be like Randy," I said, nearly puking.

"You do when it comes to his dancing."

"And don't think of it like you're being like Randy. Think of it like you're stealing his moves," Leighton said, smiling.

"Ooh, I like the sound of that."

MY MOM TOOK LEIGHTON, Sophie, Sammie, and me to see Love Puddle's performance at Sid's Stage. Sid's was a cool low-key concert venue that had made bands like Toe Gunk, Crooked Pinky and Hairy Elbow famous. I'm not sure why only bands with body parts in their names got famous at Sid's, but they did. I wondered if we should change our name or add a spleen to it or something.

We had to pay five bucks to get in. Thankfully, my Mom gave me a twenty for all of us, because I didn't carry that kind of cash around with me. After seeing Love Puddle, I wanted a refund. Everybody did. Even Randy's mother.

Sid's was a dark restaurant with brick walls and industrial lighting. The stage was kind of small, or intimate as we say in the industry, to pretend that it's not small. There were three steps up to the stage, so everyone could see the band while sitting down.

Love Puddle's manager stepped out to the stage, looking

a lot less excited than usual. Instead of yelling a big, welcoming introduction, he said, "I hope you feel the raw emotion in this performance. I think you're gonna love it. I give you Love Puddle," he said, quietly.

I looked at Sophie and shrugged.

"What's that all about?" she asked.

"No idea."

Randy walked out onto the stage, his shirt wrinkled and untucked. His hair, normally a cool kind of wild (I have to give him credit- he's got great hair), was a messy disaster. I could see his red, swelled up eyes from a few tables back.

He looked back at the rest of Love Puddle and whispered into the microphone, "Hit it."

The band started playing and for a moment, I thought they would pull it together. Randy was known for being clutch in sports. For whatever reason, it did not translate to the stage that day.

Randy started singing their hit, "Together Forever", probably a poor song choice after getting dumped by Regan. To call it singing was being kind. And he was usually a really good singer. He beat me out for the school musical. Mrs. Funderbunk thought he would be her ticket to Broadway, he was that good.

But not that day. If you hadn't seen him sing before, you might think he was trying to communicate with whales. He was totally off key, half crying, and his timing was off by a mile. His best dance move was his sway back and forth.

Leighton looked at me and said, "Don't steal any of that."

The crowd was groaning as they watched the disaster. Unlike the tomato throwers at the Outlet Center, this crowd was more shell shocked by the spectacle that was taking place. The song was slowing down. I hoped it was coming to an end.

Randy clutched the mic with two hands and sang cried, "Togeth-he-he-her forev-he-he-her." And burst into tears.

The crowd was absolutely silent.

"Poor Randy," Sammie whispered. "I just want to hold him in my arms and tell him that everything is gonna be okay."

"He's a mess," I whispered to Sophie. "This is almost sad. Almost."

"Yeah, they were terrible. I didn't know he liked Regan so much."

"I didn't know she was at all likeable," I said, shrugging.

"The guitarist was pretty rough, too. He missed a lot of notes," Sophie said. "Sly is much better."

"Don't tell Randy. He might have a breakdown."

"I haven't talked to him since the science fair."

"I wish he wouldn't talk to me," I said. "Every girl should be as smart as you."

"They should, but it's hard," Sophie said, laughing.

WE ROCKED our next gig at The Amphitheatre in front of at least a thousand people. We walked off the stage to cheers and whistles. It felt amazing. Certainly, better than getting booed and tomatoed.

As I walked down the steps and out the back of The Amphitheatre, Brody ran up to us. I looked past him and then did a double take. Calvin Conklin stood with a microphone and his camera man off in the distance.

Brody said excitedly, "Calvin wants to interview you!"

Luke said, "Oh, my God! Calvin Conklin wants to interview us?"

The band celebrated with a few pats on the back, careful not to do anything crazy, like a high-five.

Brody's face dropped. "No, he wants to interview Austin. Not the supporting cast."

"Supporting cast?" Sly asked.

"Yeah, guys. This is how it is sometimes. The singer gets more attention. It's good for the band. Be happy with that."

The rest of the crew groaned. Except for Ben. He looked kinda happy.

Ben patted me on the back and said, "Good luck, dude."

"Thanks. I'm gonna need it." Media training wasn't in the budget.

I STOOD NEXT TO CALVIN, looking up at him, not sure if I

should be looking at the camera or what. Calvin kicked it off, "Calvin Conklin here at the storied Amphitheatre with the lead Mad Man from the hot new band, Mayhem Mad Men." He looked at me and asked, "Why do you look so familiar?"

I knew it was my interview from the science fair back in school, but it went less than well, so I just looked at him with a straight face and said, "I don't know."

Calvin shrugged and continued, "Everyone wants to know, what's the inspiration for your songs, "Middle School Mayhem", "Gym Class Zero", and "Cafeteria Delirium"?"

I didn't know how to answer such an obvious question. I said, "Umm, middle school."

"Whoa, that's deep," Calvin said. "Well, you've played The Sound and now The Amphitheatre and you've been crushing the bar mitzvah scene. Tell us about how you got your start there."

"Yeah, we've kind of graduated from the bar mitzvah and birthday scene. We played a retirement home once. I mean don't get me wrong, we don't forget where we came from, but our eyes are set on the Battle of the Bands."

Calvin's eyes went wide. "Tough competition there. Do you know what you're up against? Goat Turd. I just love the sound of that," he said. "Don't you?"

"Oh, absolutely," I said. "Goat Turd is our inspiration." Yeah, I know. I could've said that better.

"Do you have a girlfriend?" Calvin asked.

"Yes, I do-"

Calvin cut me off. "Is she jealous of all the groupies?"

"We don't really have any groupies," I said. Unless you count Mr. Muscalini and he was more a motivational speaker. Most of the time, anyway.

"When are you launching your solo career?"

I raised an eyebrow. "I'm not."

"Your band mates must be upset about that."

"What? Why?"

"Because you're leaving them. You've squeezed every last drop out of their lackluster talent and now you're stepping on their backs to take your career to the next level. It's a wicked, callous power move, but I respect it. That's how I got to where I am today. Well, that and these good looks." Calvin winked at the camera and smiled. He looked back and me and said, "So tell me. What's it like having a blind drummer in your band?"

"Umm..."

The rest of the interview pretty much went like that.

I walked back to the rest of the band, shocked and upset. They sat on our equipment that was piled up on the sidewalk.

"I don't know what the heck just happened," I said, plopping to the ground.

"Nobody does. They played it to the whole crowd on the big screen," Ben said.

"You're leaving us?" Luke asked, angry. "After all we've been through? This is unbelievable."

"No, didn't you listen to what I said? Calvin is an idiot. I'm never doing another interview with him again."

"I thought it went well," Brody said, smiling.

"We need damage control," I said.

"We need a new drummer," Sly muttered.

"I'm right here," Ben said, frustrated.

"Oh, sorry. I thought you still had your headphones on."

My phone beeped. I took it out and saw a notification. It was a text from Derek. It was never a good thing to get a text from Derek, especially after being on the news. Not that it happened too often. I opened it and held my breath. And then my mouth dropped open. There was a gif of me, saying "Goat Turd is our inspiration." I dropped my phone. How the heck did he do that so quickly? I was ruined.

20

Despite the gif of me hailing Goat Turd as my inspiration, the Mayhem Mad Men continued its stratospheric rise. After rocking The Sound, we were a hot commodity. After crushing The Amphitheatre, we had a request for an out-of-state gig, which was huge. But most of our mothers wouldn't let us go. Sly was the only one who said he was in. I wasn't convinced he had even asked, but it didn't matter. We weren't going.

Unfortunately, it all started going downhill shortly after that. Because of Luke's fur-coat problem, we still played the bar mitzvah scene. It paid well even though we had outgrown them. And Temple Beth Torah was the spark that set it all off. We had a great show planned with pyrotechnics out the yin yang.

I stood in the dressing room with the rest of the group, talking to Ben. He wasn't doing well.

"Half of our school is out there. I don't want to go out there."

"Yeah, but you can barely hear them and you can't see them."

"I can't do it anymore. I'm a wreck every time."

"It'll get better," I said, not sure how it ever would. He'd been playing for weeks in front of people and he seemed to be getting worse.

Brody walked in. "It's time, guys. Let's hustle. They want "Middle School Mayhem" twice, they love it so much!"

I looked at Ben and smiled, "They love us! You wrote that song."

Ben nodded as we headed out to the stage. I eyed him to make sure he wasn't freezing up, but he seemed okay. Little did I know, it was Luke and his rapidly-growing ego that we should've been worrying about.

Everything was going well. I looked down into the crowd and saw Sophie and Sammie bouncing up and down as we started playing "Middle School Mayhem". Luke must've spotted Sophie, too, because all of a sudden, he was up at the front of the stage, mashing on the bass. I'm not gonna lie, he was playing better than ever, but I didn't need extra clutter when I was trying to dance. And I certainly didn't need what happened next.

I threw a few head nods to Luke trying to get him to go back to his spot on the stage, but he just kept getting closer. I tried to get away from him as I sang, but every step I took, he filled the gap, until I found myself on the right edge of the stage, basically wedged between his butt and a big, white pillar. Luke ripped on the bass like a mad man, staring out into the crowd in Sophie's direction.

I pushed Luke off of me with both hands, but he dug his heels in and pushed back. He was bigger than me, but I was mad. The next verse kicked in, so I kept singing while I leaned in and dug my shoulder between his shoulder blades. He squealed and gave way by a foot or so, but then pushed back.

Derek had taken enough runs at me in my lifetime that I had become pretty adept at sidestepping them, even with my limited athletic prowess. And Luke was no Derek when it came to speed, agility, or flat-out meanness.

Luke backpedaled blindly toward me, still playing. I stepped back out of his way before he connected with me and spun around him, facing the crowd, still singing. Luke crashed into the pillar. The crowd gasped as it teeter tottered. Luke turned around. Stunned, he tried to settle it, but in his rush toward it, his momentum only made it worse. He turned around for help and delivered the final death blow. The neck of his bass connected with the pillar, sending it crashing to the ground, not without first smashing the beautiful cake that probably cost more than all of Luke's fur coats, combined.

It splattered like nothing I'd ever seen, with frosting and cake filling torpedoing in every direction, including the bar mitzvah kid, Michael, and his mother. Needless to say, they didn't let the band stay for dessert.

IN LIGHT of everything that happened, we took the next day off from practice. Nobody had heard from Luke. We were all pretty mad. The rest of us even considered kicking him out of the band. He was becoming more trouble than we needed, and that wasn't even including anything to do with his admiration for Sophie, but we didn't have the heart to do it. We were just gonna have to get him under control.

Ben and I were early for the next practice at Brody's. I had to drag him there, but still he was there. And earlier than Luke. We sat with Brody in the garage, waiting for the others to arrive.

Brody said, "I'm glad you two are here. I need to talk to you about something."

I was worried that he was going to tell Ben he stunk or something. I didn't think his fragile ego could take it.

Brody looked at me and said, "Luke wants to sing."

"What?" I yelled. "After what just happened?" I was astounded.

"I think he's jealous."

"Of what?" I asked, annoyed.

"You."

"That's ridiculous. Nobody's ever jealous of me."

"You're a great singer. Getting all the attention. You've been mentioned in newspapers and been on the news with Calvin Conklin. And most important, you have the girl."

"Oh. That kinda stinks," I said, frowning. "The jealousy, not having the girl. I love the girl."

"You love the girl?" Ben asked, shocked.

Brody chimed in with an unhelpful, "Oooh."

"I- I don't know."

"Do you?" Ben asked, flabbergasted.

"I'm eleven, dude. I don't know what love is."

"You love pizza. And bacon."

"I do," I said, nodding.

"So, do you love Sophie?"

I thought about it for a moment. "I like Sophie more than bacon *on* pizza."

"Oh. My. God." Ben said. I hoped he wouldn't make a big deal over what I had just said. He jumped up and threw his hands in the air. "Dude, that's our next hit! I love you more than bacon on pizza and a glass o' chocolate milk!"

"We need to work on that, man," I said. I was just glad he moved onto a different subject.

A car pulled up into the driveway. Just Charles and Luke hopped out and grabbed their stuff out of the trunk.

Brody looked at me and said, "I told Luke, 'no' about the singing, but I just thought you should know what's up."

"Thanks."

Sly pulled up on the street and joined the rest of the crew. The three of them walked up the driveway to the open garage.

"What's up, guys?" Brody said.

"I'll tell you what's up," Just Charles said. His face showed his anger, but I didn't know why. Normally, he was pretty chill. Just Charles nearly tossed his keyboard off to the side.

"What's going on?" I asked.

"I'll tell you what's going on," Just Charles said.

"What's the deal, man?" Ben asked.

"I'll tell you what's the deal, man!"

See, I told you. He didn't even know how to be mad.

"So, can you just say it already?" Brody asked.

Just Charles said, "We should have food for the band, friends, and family after each gig. And I think we should have fresh-cut flowers, too."

Oh, God. The fame was getting to Just Charles, too. This was bad.

"Since when do you like flowers? Actually, aren't you allergic to flowers?" Ben asked.

"I don't like them and yes, I'm allergic, but I want them anyway."

"Yeah, and I want an after party!" Luke said, pointing to Brody. "And you need to get me a fur coat sponsorship. Those things are really expensive!"

"So, stop wearing them," I said. "In the summer."

"Okay, but the after party is still a good idea, right?" Luke asked.

Brody looked at them, dumbfounded. "You guys are in the sixth grade."

"Going into seventh," Luke said, defensively.

"Oh, right. That changes things." Brody tapped his chin. "What do you want?"

Luke looked at Just Charles and said, "I don't know. A lot of pizza and juice boxes."

"Juice boxes?" Just Charles asked.

"No, lemonade. And soda, man. Not the diet kind, either," Luke said.

"This is ridiculous," Sly said.

"One more thing! I want a headset," Luke said, smiling.

"A headset?" Ben asked.

"Yeah, like one of those hands-free microphones."

"You don't even sing!" Sly said.

"Maybe that should change," Luke said, looking at me.

"Maybe you should figure out how to play the bass and

not cost us more money in damage than we get paid before you take on new challenges," I said, icily.

"Big words from a little boy," Luke said, stepping toward me.

"I got more than words for you," I said, pounding my fist into my palm.

We were about have our first band mate brawl.

21

Every good band has a brawl. You knock each other's teeth out and then you bond like brothers. Or at least that's what Brody tried to tell us.

Luke and I stared at each other, nose to nose. He was a bit taller than me, so I had to put my head back a little bit, but still.

"Come on, guys," Ben said. "Knock it off."

Brody countered, "Just let it happen. We need this. We'll come out stronger."

My eyes bore into Luke's. 'You wanna dance, skinny boy?" I asked, adrenaline surging through my veins.

"It's on like Donkey Kong!" Luke yelled.

Neither of us moved. I assessed his weaknesses. I wasn't sure if he was gonna get the Kung-Fu kick or the devastating Camel Clutch. Nobody likes a Kung-Fu kick to the face, but the Camel Clutch was demoralizing and Luke needed an ego check. I decided to surprise him with a fake out.

"You eat breakfast yet?" I asked, menacingly.

"Yeah," he said, surprised. "An omelet with bacon. It was spectacular."

"Oh, that sounds good," I said.

"Why do you look disappointed?"

"I was gonna ask if you wanted to eat my foot," I said.
"Well, do you, punk?"

"Dude, that's kinda gross," Just Charles said.

"I didn't mean, like put syrup on it. I meant a Kung-Fu
kick." I stepped back and got into a karate stance. I hoped he
didn't know I had never taken a day of karate in my life.

"Bring it, Davenfart."

"Oh, no you didn't! Only Randy's allowed to call me
that!" I yelled, charging like a bull in slow motion. Well, it
was my regular speed, but it looked slow motion. "Ahhhh!"

Luke responded, surging toward me, slapping and flap-
ping his wrists like a T-Rex trying to play the bongo drums.

"Ha ha!" I yelled as I slapped his hand to the side and
circled around behind him like a cat. "You fell for the oldest
trick in the book!" I wrapped my arms around him from
behind, trying to force him to the ground so I could imple-
ment the demoralizing Camel Clutch.

"What's that?" Luke asked, struggling to break my
concrete-like grip.

"The fake Kung-Fu kick, Camel Clutch attack, of course!"

"Get off of me!"

We continued to struggle, neither of us gaining any ground on the other.

"The Camel Clutch is on the menu, Lukey!" I yelled, trying to force him to the ground.

After a while, it just felt like I was just hugging him instead of fighting.

"Hey, you're kinda warm. That feels good," Luke said. "Like when my Mom puts my blankie in the dryer before I go to bed."

"You have a blankie?" I asked. I couldn't fight someone with a blankie. It just wasn't right.

"No!" Luke said, defensively.

I didn't believe him, so I let him go. Luke straightened out his shirt and walked away. Just Charles followed him. Ben just kind of stood on the side, not sure what to do.

"Well, glad we worked that out," Brody said, smiling. "Now, back to practice." Luke and Just Charles disappeared around the side of the house. "After a few minute break," Brody added.

I looked at Ben and said, "That went well, I think."

Ben looked shell shocked. He was not in his normal stone mode, but it was close.

Sly pulled me aside and whispered, "This group is falling apart. We need to fix it."

"What do you mean? We just worked it out. Did you see that? What's the matter now?" I asked.

"You know what's the matter," Sly said, his hands on his hips.

"No, that's why I asked," I said, annoyed.

"Well, you should know. Turn around once in a while when you're on stage and see how our drummer is doing."

"This again?" He was bashing Ben. Again.

Sly wasn't finished. "And while we're on it, the other two should probably go, too. They goin' cuckoo with the fame. Or maybe you haven't noticed with all your own fame, you know, interviews and all."

"They'll get used to it. Why do you want to change anything? They're my friends. And everybody loves us."

THE NEXT DAY AT CAMP, everything seemed fine. There was no fighting, faux fur coats, or threats of Kung-Fu. Our group was assembled and ready to go. Luke and I were fine. Or at least seemed to be. And then things got interesting.

Brody ran into camp like a wacko. "We're goin' to the beach!"

"Nobody told us anything about a field trip today," I said, looking around at the rest of the crew. "Did you guys know about this?"

Everyone shook their heads.

"No, no, no," Brody said. "I've got a surprise for you! We got a gig at Beach Blast!" Brody threw two handfuls of something up in the air.

We all looked up and then screamed in pain as sand rained down upon our faces and embedded under our eyelids, up our noses, and in our mouths.

"Ahh! What's that in my eyes?" I yelled.

"It's sand!" Brody said, excitedly.

"Why the heck are you throwing sand in our eyes?" Ben asked. "Why does the universe hate me? Where are my glaucoma shades when I need them?"

"We got a gig at Beach Blast! Yeah!" Brody said, seemingly not caring at all that he had blinded the entire band. It wouldn't change much of Ben's performance, since we already covered his eyes, but the rest of us would be in trouble, me in particular. I could barely stay on the stage when I could actually see the ground in front of me.

My mom was picking up Derek, Leighton, and me after Leighton was done cleaning up at camp. I leaned up against a tree, reading an e-book. I heard footsteps. I looked up, thinking it was Derek about to smash a pie in my face, but it was Regan. I looked back down at my story, not realizing that she was walking over to talk to me.

"Hey there, Austin," Regan said, sweetly.

I looked back up and scanned the grounds, checking to see if there were kids around, perhaps one named Austin. I was the one she was talking to, so I racked my brain, trying to figure out what prank Regan was about to play on me.

Regan looked down at me. "I hear you're playing Beach Blast. Wow. That's amazing."

"Yeah, we're very excited," I said monotone, looking back down at my story.

"I'm sorry I was a jerk. I misjudged you and your friends. I didn't realize how cool you were, and talented."

"Thanks," I said, a little confused. I wasn't sure if she was being serious or reeling me in. I figured I would give her the benefit of the doubt, plus it felt good for someone so popular to show interest in me. I know. I know. She wasn't nice, but you don't always think of that in the moment. When she was saying those things, I forgot that she was mean. I only remembered that she was popular.

"Well, I gotta go. Maybe, I'll come see you play at Beach Blast."

"Uh, sure," I said. "It's gonna be a blast," I said, stupidly.

~

BEACH BLAST LIVED up to its name. It was on the beach and it was a blast. All the bands got to hang out, eating BBQ, and partying it up on the beach, while we all watched the other bands play. Most of the other bands were high school and college kids, so they mainly kept to themselves, but we just had fun being a part of it all.

The Mayhem Mad Men sat in beach chairs in a circle. I excused myself to go the little boys' room. The iced tea was flowing at Beach Blast. I half expected Max to be running it when I got there. No such luck. When I got back, I almost lost my marbles.

Sophie and Luke were talking, no, arguing. She seemed a lot angrier than him. Luke leaned down toward her. Sophie pushed Luke with both hands. He shook his head and walked away.

I ran over to Sophie. "Are you okay? What happened?"

"No, he tried to kiss me," Sophie said, angrily.

That was the final straw. I felt the anger build up inside me. It must've been how Bruce Banner felt every time he turned into the Hulk. I just hoped I wasn't green. I didn't think it would be a good look for me. I stared at Luke as he walked away.

"Let him go," Just Charles said.

"No. He just tried to kiss my girlfriend! He's supposed to be my friend." I started running through what felt like quick sand.

I caught up to Luke. I was fuming. "What was that all about?" I yelled.

He just shrugged.

"Really? That's all you have to say? A whole lot of nothing?"

"I'm sorry. I didn't mean for it to happen."

"You tried to kiss her. It didn't look like an accident."

I mean, I just like her. It just happened. I don't know what else to say."

"I don't know how you could do it. We were supposed to be friends."

"We are friends."

"I don't think so."

I walked back to the band while Sly stormed off.

He looked at me and said, "I quit."

"What the heck?"

Ben was walking my way. I asked, "What the heck happened with him?

Ben said, "You don't want to know."

I walked back to Sophie and said, "What happened now?"

"He asked me if I could ever like him. I told him I liked you. He got mad. I got mad at him for being a bad friend. And then he walked away, which I'm going to do."

Sophie walked off.

"Don't go," I said.

"Please, just give me a minute," Sophie said.

"Where are you going?"

"Anywhere, but here. I need to be by myself."

IT WAS GAME TIME. And we had no team. We were scrambling to find Luke and Sly. I couldn't find Sophie anywhere and she wasn't answering her phone. Just Charles had given me a copy of the music and I was trying to learn the guitar part. I could play a little bit, but I wasn't very good. I certainly wasn't Beach Blast good an hour before the show.

Brody walked over, a broad smile on his face. He looked around, confused. "Where is everyone?"

I stood up and asked, "Where the heck have you been? Our whole band just fell apart."

Ben chimed in, "Well, to be accurate and true to Nerd Nation, 40% of our band."

"What?" Brody said, the color in his face evaporating. "It's Beach Blast! This is big time!"

"You have to tell them we can't play," I said, taking a deep breath. "It's over."

"I'm not telling them that. You guys are going to play!" Brody yelled.

"How? Luke and Sophie aren't here and they're the only two who can play bass. Sly isn't here to play guitar and I stink at it," I said.

"Well, you're gonna have to stink it up out there on your own," Brody said.

"Why don't you play?" Ben asked.

"I can't play the guitar," he said, defensively.

I yelled, "Neither can I!"

"You're the leader. You gotta do what you gotta do," Brody said. "Strap in. It's gonna be a bumpy ride."

"Thanks for the support," I said.

I took a deep breath and looked at Ben, as he was fiddling with a pink sleep mask.

"Dude, what the heck is that?" I asked.

"What, this? It's my mother's sleeping mask. It keeps the light out in the morning, so she can sleep better." Ben said.

"Yeah, I figured that, but what are you doing with it?"

"I'm going to use it instead of the bandana. It's more comfortable."

Ben slipped on the sleep mask, looking quite ridiculous, and then popped on his glaucoma shades on top of them. He looked the furthest thing from a rock star. But it was the least of my worries.

I led him over to the drums and sat him in his seat. Brody was right behind me as I turned around and handed me a guitar.

"Good luck," he said.

I was going to need it. The good news was that I could rock out on the guitar and not have to dance around with the mic. I could only stand in front of the mic, play the guitar, and sing. And if I wasn't singing, I would still have the guitar to keep me from dancing. I kind of liked the idea, although I wasn't actually worrying about how the guitar would sound.

I stood in front of the microphone stand, the guitar strapped across my shoulder, as I looked out at the thousands of people gathered along the beach, most of them looking back at me. I turned around and shrugged at Just Charles. Ben couldn't see a thing, so I gave Just Charles a nod.

Just Charles kicked his foot out behind him, tapping the drums.

Ben nodded in Just Charles' direction and yelled, "One, two, three!" and kicked off "Cafeteria Delirium."

Just Charles and I joined in. I felt pretty good about my guitar playing, but the crowd didn't seem to be feeling it. I saw more people yawning and scratching their heads than cheering. We were bombing. I hoped that once I got into the lyrics, the crowd's energy would pick up. I also hoped they didn't have any tomatoes in their coolers.

I kicked into the lyrics, "It's the middle of the school day and you're feeling kinda hungraaaay, so you head down to the cafeteria with a little bit of fear in ya. Waitin' on the lunch line, you gotta close your eyes. You don't want to see what's in the Seafood Surprise. How old are those moldy buns? Last week I got the runs. I got cafeteria delirium!"

The crowd's energy was growing. And then I heard a bass start ripping behind me. I turned around to see Luke walking across the stage, nodding his head to the beat. My heart stopped feeling like it was going to implode. For a minute, I felt pretty good and thought with Luke back that we would actually be okay. I was very wrong.

Ben jumped on the rhythm of the bass, his timing on the drums catching up. Just Charles continued wailing on the keyboards as usual, but Luke's return seemed to give him a boost of energy. And then I had to go and ruin it all.

In my excitement, I decided to add a little spice to the song. In between verses, I had some time I didn't need to stay chained to the microphone. Feeling the music, I spun around wildly playing the guitar. I figured if I couldn't play it that well, I might as well at least try to look good doing it.

The neck of the guitar caught the microphone pole and sent it flying sideways across the stage toward the side. Feedback echoed through the speakers as the microphone rolled under the curtain. I tried to maintain my coolness, playing the guitar as I headed over to the microphone. I bent down to pick up the mic and fumbled for it. The song was going downhill. I couldn't play the guitar while reaching for the mic. I could barely play without having to do nerd yoga (bending over). I wrapped my fingers around the mic and stood up. I bumped into something and nearly fell, but hurried back to the microphone stand and picked it up.

I looked out at the crowd. They were all just staring at the mess I had made. Well, I blame it on Luke for leaving, but as far as they were concerned, it was my fault. And then Brody went and made it worse.

As I started to sing the next verse, I looked over at Brody who counted down on his fingers from three to one, and then pressed the pyrotechnics button. The Sparkulars exploded out of their tubes.

The crowd roared. Thankfully, it seemed to get the crowd engaged again as I sang, "I think something just moved in my chocolate mousse. Potatoes O'gratin, smellin' kinda rotten. Chicken nuggets knocked my front tooth loose. Eww, this has snot in it, the soup is made of goop and the beef stew tastes like poop!"

I looked out at the crowd and they were all yelling at me and pointing to the stage. Smoke surged from the curtain near a fallen Sparkular. Flames were starting to rise up the curtain. I must have knocked it over when I got the mic.

Luke and Just Charles didn't know what to do. Luke ran over to Just Charles' side of the stage, away from the flames, while Ben had no idea what was going on and his drums were on fire. He wailed on them and the crowd roared. With the sleep mask, glaucoma shades, and the headphones, he couldn't see or hear any of what was going on. I didn't know why he didn't smell the smoke, but perhaps he thought he was playing so hard the sticks were smoking.

I dropped the mic (a bad mic drop) and rushed to the back of the stage. Ben's drum sticks had caught fire. They were dwindling by the second. Two inches of the sticks broke off in a charred mess as Ben continued to play. The sad part is that it was one of his best drum solos. He was really feeling it. Sly wouldn't have wanted to kick Ben out of the band had he always played like he was playing at that moment.

But it had to come to an end. I didn't want Ben's finest band moment to be his final life moment. I tore off the glaucoma shades and the sleep mask. Ben looked at me confused as he continued to play and then his eyes bulged as he saw his drum sticks half-eaten by fire.

Ben's face morphed to fear. I could see his muscles start to tense up. We had to get out of there.

I looked at Luke and Just Charles and yelled, "Help me! We have to carry him!"

The three of us grabbed our statuesque drummer and friend and lifted him off the stool. We waddled away as Brody rushed across the stage, blasting everything and everyone in sight with a fire extinguisher. As if it wasn't bad enough that our performance had ended with an unplanned fire evacuation, the spray engulfed my face like a tornado of exploding foam. It was like a pie to the face times a thousand. Not that Derek has ever smashed a pie in my face...

As we made our way off the stage, carrying Ben to safety, Sophie, Sammie, and other bands rushed over to us to help. A few college kids grabbed Ben and carried him by his wrists and ankles to the back of the stage.

"Are you okay?" Sophie yelled, frantic.

"I'm fine," I said, as we all looked at Ben laying on the sand, staring up at the blue sky.

"Ben?" I yelled.

Sophie echoed with another, "Ben?"

Just Charles and I knelt down beside him and shook him. "You okay?"

"Yep," he said. "Well, I will be when I move to Canada. I've always wanted a pet moose."

"I hate to burst your bubble, buddy, but I don't think anybody has a pet moose."

"My whole life is ruined," Ben muttered.

"Because you can't have a pet moose?" I asked.

Ben didn't answer. He rolled to his side, sat up, and said, "I'm done with this. I hate it. I hate being this way. I'm sorry, but I quit."

Ben stood up, wiped the sand off, and walked away, leaving us all speechless.

"Well, that could've gone worse," Just Charles said, patting me on the shoulder.

"Really? How? We don't have a drummer. Or a guitarist."

Luke chimed in, "Yeah, and two of us like the same girl."

I just looked at him and shook my head. "Really, dude?"

22

I was worried about Ben. He hadn't answered any of my calls or texts. My mother had spoken to his mother and she said that he grabbed a half gallon of ice cream and disappeared into his room for the rest of the night, so I knew it wasn't good. Ben was a stress ice cream eater.

He didn't show up for camp the next day, either. Luke, Just Charles, Teddy, and I sat around the pool, waiting for Brody to show up. And maybe even Sly.

"I guess Sly's not coming," Luke said.

"Good," I said. "He's an idiot. With friends like him, who needs an enemy like Randy Warblemacher?"

It was as if I summoned my evil nemesis by speaking his name. Randy walked by on his way to his group and called out to me, "Hey, Davenfart, I heard your gig went well at Beach Blast! You really set the place on fire," he said, laughing.

I had no comeback. There was no coming back from that. Mayhem Mad Men had burned to ashes. Almost literally.

Brody walked out of the utility room and over to us. He had a pained look on his face.

"What's the matter?" I asked.

"I just had a meeting with Quackenbush. Sly's leaving."

"Leaving camp?" Ben asked.

"Our group. Both of them."

"He's leaving Mayhem Mad Men?" Luke asked.

"It gets worse. I saw him wearing a Love Puddle shirt."

"No!" I yelled.

"What the heck is that all about?" Ben asked.

"He's just trying to make us angry," Just Charles said.

"No, I think he joined their band," Brody said.

And then Regan walked by. She looked at me and then looked away and said, "Eww. I can't believe I ever thought you were cool."

"Good seeing you, too," I said, jokingly, even though it hurt. I felt like everybody whoever watched us play probably felt the same way that Regan felt.

WE WERE all moping around like somebody had died. I guess somebody did. Or something. Our band. Our dreams of superstardom. The idea that we could somehow transform from nerd to cool. It was all just a cruel tease. Like Regan's fake kiss with Ben.

Brody was the worst of us. He had failed before with French Lisp and thought Mayhem Mad Men would redeem him, but he had no such luck. He sat with his back up against a tree as we sat around doing nothing. I think we were supposed to be at an underwater basket weaving class or something, but none of us could hold our breath for that long. Or weave baskets.

Brody whispered, "I miss the good ole days, man. When we dove off stages and crushed old ladies. When we lit the stage on fire and almost ourselves. When we wore faux fur and felt good about ourselves."

"And we turned Love Puddle's keyboard into a fart machine," I added.

"I miss the limelight," Just Charles said.

"I loved the limelight," Luke said. "And faux fur. I'm gonna have to cancel that fur coat shipment from China I ordered last week. I gotta tell you, though, the bulk discounts are amazing."

Is it crazy that I still want to win Battle of the Bands?" I asked.

"What are we gonna do?" Just Charles asked.

"There's only one thing left to do," I said, standing up and pounding my hand into my fist. "We gotta get the band back together!"

"But how?" Luke asked.

"No clue."

We had no idea. Like none.

I LAY on the couch in my den, watching YouTube videos of cool bands, trying to pick up some dancing tips. We still didn't have a band. I hadn't even talked to Ben, let alone convinced him to come back. We were also still short a guitarist and we had no plans of asking Sly back. There was no coming back from joining the enemy, Love Puddle.

My dad walked into the den with something folded in his hand.

"What's that?" I asked.

"A newspaper article," he answered.

"What's that?" I laughed, making fun of my brother.

"Your brother," my dad said, shaking his head and chuckling.

"But this is about you." My dad unfolded the paper and started to read, "Mayhem Mad Men is a talented band. There is no doubt that they have their kinks to work out, but with experience, they will be playing for crowds for years to come."

"The band broke up," I said.

"What? But you guys are so good."

"I want to get the band back together, but I don't think I can. Ben has stage fright and doesn't want to play anymore. Sly is gone and I don't want him back. And Luke tried to kiss Sophie. I'm not sure I want him, either."

"That's Rock 'n Roll, man," my dad said. I had no idea what he was talking about. "What can you do to help Ben?"

"Well, the first thing is to get him to stop gorging on ice cream. His mother told me he's been swimming in it. Can you take me over to Scoops?"

MY DAD PULLED the car into the parking lot at Scoops and rolled to a stop. He looked at me and said, "Good luck. And get me a sundae with hot fudge and colored sprinkles."

"What flavor?"

"Cotton candy. No, birthday cake. No, rum raisin. Black raspberry. That's the one. Or all of them!"

"Okay, Dad. How do you expect me to pay for all of this?" I asked with my hand out.

"Here's a twenty. Buy yourself something, too. And keep this between us."

I grabbed the twenty and hopped out. "Thanks."

I walked around the corner to the front of the shop. Ben was sitting on the short wall, chowing down on a large sundae. Well, actually scraping the bottom of a formerly large sundae.

I sat down next to him. He greeted me with a burp. It was a good one. One of his best ever.

"That was sweet, dude." I thought he might need a confidence boost. He always had a lot of pride in his burping.

"Thanks," he said, stone faced. It was bad if he wasn't proud of his burp.

"I'm sorry you're upset. What's going on?" I asked, stupidly.

"I made a fool of myself. And I stunk," he said, simply.

"I stink at a lot of things," I said.

"Not helping."

"I'm sorry. I just think we all cared too much about what everyone else thought about us."

"I just felt like I was fake, like why would anyone care what I could do or what we had to say?" Ben said.

"Because we were good. I think you're the first drummer to ever play with sticks on fire," I said, chuckling.

"You're not helping. That wasn't on purpose. What are we gonna do?"

"Go back to being weird, I guess. It stinks, but we've lived with it all these years."

"It's not that bad. All these clowns are gonna work for us someday. That's the only good thing about being a nerd. Eventually, you win. At least that's what my dad says."

"Then why have you run through two loyalty cards? That's like twenty hole punches, dude. That's a lot of ice cream."

"Someday is not today. I'm just tired of being a loser. Of not mattering."

"You're not a loser. With or without the band. You're my best friend and you matter to me."

We sat there for a minute without talking before I asked, "You wanna head back? My dad is in the car."

"Nah, I want another Sundae. I'm eating my feelings. My mom would have a heart attack if she heard that, but whatever."

"She knows. She told me you were here."

"I just wish I could play without being afraid," Ben said, frustrated.

"You should get some sort of shock therapy. Ask your parents. Maybe for your birthday."

"I was thinking more like hypnosis."

"Yeah, that actually sounds better. Sorry, dude. I'm not a professional. Do you think you're ever gonna get back out there? Like before Battle of the Bands starts?" I asked.

"I'm done. Battle of the Bands isn't happening for me." Ben said. "Sorry."

"It's okay," I said, disappointed. "Then I guess we're done. It was a great run."

"Was it?"

"Some of it was. But then it stopped being fun. You know, with the friction with you and Sly, Luke and me."

"I never had fun. Well, only the songwriting and practicing. The performing, no," Ben said.

"Kind of a problem."

"And one I don't know how to fix. Or if I even want to."

"I hear you. You coming back to camp soon? Everybody misses you. And Sly left our group."

"He did?"

"Yep. Joined Love Puddle."

"Oh, wow. Yeah, I guess I'll come back if he's not there. Love Puddle. Now, it's Hate Puddle," Ben said, laughing.

"Nice one," I said, lying. I didn't want to hurt his fragile confidence.

After I got my dad's sundae and left Ben alone with his next one, I walked back to the parking lot. A tall kid with messy hair and ripped jeans bounced around the corner like he was on a pogo stick.

"Whoa, dude! Sorry," he said. He looked at me and asked, "Aren't you the lead singer of Mayhem Mad Men?"

I smiled weakly. "I was," I said, continuing on my way.

"Wait, what? Hold on. What do you mean, was? You guys are awesome!"

I stopped and turned around. "We kinda broke up or did."

"Say it ain't so, man! But, if we had you, we would be sick!"

"Who is you?" I asked.

The kid stepped toward me and put out his hand for a shake. "I'm Josh, the bassist for Plumber's Crack."

Another one of those ridiculous names. "Cool. I've heard of you guys."

"Dude, we need a lead singer. We lost our singer at the beginning of the summer. It hasn't been the same since then. We can't do Battle of the Bands unless you join us."

"I don't know. I'm not sure I'm ready for that," I said. I liked being in a band with my friends. I wasn't sure I wanted to join a new band, although the idea of playing in Battle of the Bands was kinda cool.

"Look us up online. Call the phone number. It's mine. Tell me by Monday. Plumberscrack.com."

I took a deep breath. "Okay, I'll check it out."

"Yeah, dude!" Josh said, excitedly. "Think about it." He put his hand out for another shake. I grabbed it and shook. Josh proceeded to do a whole bunch of different shakes, grabs, smacks, and twists, none of which I knew or could keep up with. It was almost worse than my high-fiving.

"We'll work on that, man. Catch you later! Yeah!" Josh said with a wave. "Call me Monday," he said without looking back.

I stood there for a minute, just thinking. And then realized my dad's ice cream was melting, so I hurried back.

I WAS TORN. For the next two days, my mind was on Plumber's Crack. I know, a weird thing to think about. After lunch on Monday at camp, I walked with Sophie for a few minutes. We ended up bumping into Zorch, who was emptying trash around the grounds.

Zorch looked up when he saw footsteps approaching.

"Hey! How's it going?" and then when he looked closer, asked, "Why so glum?"

"Our band broke up after a terrible performance. We were kind of falling apart for a few performances."

Zorch stepped closer. "What happened? Greed? Ego? Women?"

I looked at Sophie. "Kinda," I said.

"That's how it happens every time," he said, shaking his head. "You can't take your focus off the love of making music, man."

"I was offered an opportunity to be the lead singer of Plumber's Crack."

Zorch chuckled. "Wow, you really hit the jackpot. Or crackpot."

"Very funny," I said, while Sophie chuckled.

"I looked them up online. They've had some serious gigs. Their lead singer got grounded for his last report card and had to drop out. If I joined them, I could still compete in the battle."

"But what about the rest of the guys? You're not the kinda kid to leave your mates behind."

I shrugged. "Ben is out for good. Luke is, well, I'm mad at Luke."

"You're just gonna leave Just Charles?" Sophie asked.

"If I join Plumber's Crack, at least I get to hit the battle. If I don't, neither of us do."

"Tough choice, kid. That's above my pay grade. Good luck with it."

Yeah, thanks for the help, I thought.

23

It was after lunch and Ben still wasn't at camp. I thought he would eventually show up. I was back with my group, well, without Sly and Ben.

Just Charles nodded to me. "Where's Ben?"

"Haven't seen him. He was pretty depressed yesterday. He probably skipped. I'll check in with him later. He said he was coming back, though."

"He hasn't called me back."

"I had to track him down at Scoops."

"That must've been bad." Just Charles chuckled.

"You have no idea." My pulse quickened as I thought about telling Just Charles about my new offer. "Hey, I wanted to tell you." I took a deep breath and said, "I was asked to join Plumber's Crack, a pretty solid band."

"Oh," Just Charles said, disappointed. "Okay. I guess I was still wishing we could get back together."

"Sly's gone and Ben said he doesn't want to come back. And I'm still kinda mad at Luke."

Just Charles nodded. "Do they need a keyboardist?"

I shrugged. "I don't know for certain, but I don't think so."

"Oh."

My stomach was in knots.

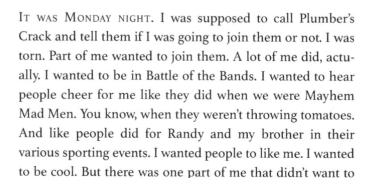

I<small>T WAS</small> M<small>ONDAY NIGHT</small>. I was supposed to call Plumber's Crack and tell them if I was going to join them or not. I was torn. Part of me wanted to join them. A lot of me did, actually. I wanted to be in Battle of the Bands. I wanted to hear people cheer for me like they did when we were Mayhem Mad Men. You know, when they weren't throwing tomatoes. And like people did for Randy and my brother in their various sporting events. I wanted people to like me. I wanted to be cool. But there was one part of me that didn't want to join them: my heart.

I'm sure that sounds all cheesy and stuff, but it was true. It didn't feel right. I didn't know anything about Plumber's Crack. And I didn't want to know. I had no desire to explore Plumber's Crack. I decided I was either going to play with my crew or not play at all.

I texted Ben, Just Charles, and Luke. 'My house. One hour. You in?'

Just Charles responded within a minute. 'Yep.'

And then Luke, 'K'. Would it kill the kid to put an 'O' in front of the 'K'? Is he really that lazy? I just don't get it.

Sorry to digress. Moving on. Ben never responded. Just Charles and Luke arrived together and early. I sat on a lounge chair in my back yard, staring up into the blue sky as they approached from behind me.

I stood up and gave Just Charles a fist bump. They were more controllable than high-fives. True, a punch hurts more than a slap, but I felt like there was a much lower risk of a fist bump going wrong.

I looked at Luke. He was staring at the ground. "Hey," I said.

Luke looked up at me and said, "I'm so sorry. I don't know what got into me. I was an idiot."

"Yep."

"I am going to apologize to Sophie, too."

"That better be all you do," I said.

"I deserved that."

"So, what's the deal?" Just Charles asked. "Why the meeting?"

"We're getting the band back together. I mean, if you guys want to. No gigs, just fun. Otherwise, Ben will spontaneously self-combust."

"Where's Ben?" Luke asked.

"Dunno. Didn't respond."

"That's not good."

"I haven't seen him since Scoops. I think he'll like this idea, though."

"I do," Just Charles said.

"It's about us, playing together. It's about the music. If Ben can't play in front of people, we'll lose the people and just have fun."

"I thought it was about the girls and being cool?" Luke asked, disappointed.

"Not anymore," I said.

"Just for the fun of it," Luke said, trying to absorb it. "With you guys? I can handle that."

"We still need a guitarist," Just Charles said.

"Luke, why don't you play it and we'll drop the bass. You said you didn't like it, anyway, and we're not performing."

"Nah, man. I kinda like it. It's the glue that keeps the band together."

"Says the guy who nearly broke up the band," I said, chuckling.

"I guess I deserve that, too." Luke thought for a moment. "It might be a bad time for this, but what about Sophie?"

I liked the idea of playing with Sophie, but not if it made Luke go bonkers.

Luke looked at me and said, "It's your call."

BEN HAD BEEN MISSING in action for too long. It wasn't like him. Normally, when one of us got knocked down, embarrassed, or both, we took it as a team. Kind of like when both of us got pushed into the pool. I did that for him, just so you know. This time, he was going it alone, which made me nervous. I'm just glad he wasn't lactose intolerant.

I walked over to Ben's house and knocked on the door. It opened with a creak, revealing Mrs. Gordon, a tall, thin woman with short hair and glasses.

"Hi, Austin," she said.

"Hi, Mrs. Gordon. I really need to talk to Ben. I know he's been upset and probably wants to be alone, but I'm afraid he's going to burn his college fund at Scoops."

"Me, too," she said. "But I think he's much better. Why don't you go up to his room and knock?"

"Okay, thanks," I said, scooting past her and up the stairs.

I knocked on Ben's door, which had a bunch of pictures of our crew together and some super hero stuff. I chose to knock on Cyclops from X-Men, because I just didn't like him and wanted to punch him in the head. Ben and I don't always agree on everything. If we don't agree, it's usually about comics.

"You may enter," he said in a monotone voice.

I opened the door and peeked in, not sure if I would recognize him after all the ice cream he scarfed down over the past few days. And what I saw was very surprising.

Ben sat in the the pretzel position or crisscross applesauce, if you prefer, with his eyes closed, meditating.

I tiptoed in, not sure what I was interrupting.

"Greetings, my friend," Ben said without opening his eyes.

"How did you know it was me?" I asked. "I didn't say a word and your eyes are closed."

"I felt your presence and only you would knock directly on Cyclops, an uninformed move, but I forgive you."

I just scratched my head. I had no idea how to respond. Ben opened his eyes and stood up.

"Dude, where have you been?" I asked.

He thought for a moment. "Max Mulvihill's," he said, uncertain. Like I wouldn't believe him or something.

"You know Max?" I asked, surprised.

"Yes. You do, too?" he asked, relieved. I'm not crazy?" Ben asked.

I wondered if I was crazy, too. I never talked about Max Mulvihill's bathroom to anyone. I half believed it was fake and that I was crazy. I could never get up the courage to tell anyone that I actually knew about it. I mean, who would really believe that some dude ran a private bathroom within a public middle school that had massage chairs and tables, disco balls, video games, and artisanal cheeses? It was ridiculous.

"What were you doing there?" I asked.

"Emptying my mind. Feeding my soul. Becoming one with the universe."

"You did all that at Max's? How long were you there for?"

"I don't know. Eight hours?" Ben said, shrugging.

"You did all that in eight hours?" I asked, my voice rising by an octave.

"No, that was just like the first hour. The rest of the time, we played Snooker."

"What the heck is that?"

"Snooker is a cue sport which originated among British Army officers stationed in India in the latter half of the 19th century."

"Oh, yeah. That's right," I said, having no idea what it was. "Wait, he cured you in an hour?"

"He runs a full-service operation," Ben said, simply.

"That he does," I said, nodding. "Regardless, I think we should keep our knowledge of the man to ourselves for security purposes."

"Absolutely."

"So, kind of a lot's happened since you became one with the universe."

"Whatever it is, I am one with it," Ben said.

I thought he might be getting a little carried away with it all, but I ignored it. "I worked everything out with the rest of the guys. Minus Sly. He's a punk."

"I never liked that kid," Ben said angrily, "But I forgive him," he added quickly.

"Well, you kinda did until he didn't like you."

"I am at peace with that, my friend. And I am in."

"In what?" I asked, confused.

"Mayhem Mad Men and Battle of the Bands."

"You are?"

"Most definitely. I didn't tell you something about my time with Max."

"What's that?"

"I am also one with the drums."

24

J ust Charles, Luke, and I walked into camp. I was nervous, because Ben wasn't on the bus again. He said he was coming back and he seemed to be over all of his issues. I hoped he hadn't relapsed and hit the breakfast buffet at Scoops. I wasn't sure they had one, but still.

"I thought you said Ben was coming?" Just Charles asked.

"He did say that. I don't know what's going on. I'm surprised he's not here," I said.

As we walked down the path toward the common area, the three of us almost fell over each other. Ben sat atop a knee-high boulder in the lotus position with his eyes closed and hands folded in his lap.

"What the-" Luke said.

"I dare you to mess with him," Just Charles said to Luke.

"No way. You do it."

"Okay, I'll do it, baby." Just Charles slinked up to Ben. Before Just Charles could do anything, Ben grabbed Just Charles' hand, bent it backward, swept his feet from underneath him, and returned them to the Lotus position without effort.

Just Charles hit the ground with a thud. I shook my head, hoping to get my brain working again. I didn't believe what I had just witnessed. Ben's eyes were still closed.

Ben opened his eyes and hopped down from the boulder. "Namaste, my brothers," he said, bowing with his hands in the prayer position. "I hope this glorious morning is treating you well. Except for you, Just Charles. I assume that hurt."

"You got that right," Just Charles said, rubbing his hip.

"Why weren't you on the bus?" I asked.

"I walked here. It focuses the mind. Nurtures the spirit. And I missed the bus," he said, chuckling.

Brody and Mr. Muscalini walked up to us. Mr. Muscalini stepped forward. He looked at us solemnly. His eyes were red and puffy.

"Brody, my boy, told me about the bad news. I'm disappointed-"

"Mr. Muscalini-" I said.

He cut me off. "Let me finish. Gentlemen, you moved me. "Gym Class Zero" caused me to question my entire career. My life's mission. I am forever changed. I didn't understand the challenges you faced." Mr. Muscalini started to choke up. "And as for the band, you have a gift. And you need to share it. Davenport," he said, pointing to me. "You have the voice of an angel. You hit high notes that even six-year-old girls can't hit."

"Umm, thank you?' I said, not sure it was actually a compliment, at least the second part.

Mr. Muscalini continued, "And Gordo when nobody's looking, you're amazing."

"Thanks, I guess."

"And you two," he said, looking at Just Charles and Luke. "I'm not sure what you guys do, but you look good doing it. That faux fur is spectacular. I gotta get me some of that. You think they make an athletic fit for these biceps?" Mr. Muscalini flexed and admired his bulging muscles.

"Not sure, sir," Luke said. "But I know of a custom place in L.A. that might be able to help."

"Nice," Mr. Muscalini said. "Where was I?" he asked.

"Umm, the band," Brody said.

"Right, thanks, son." Mr. Muscalini patted Brody on the shoulder, who just shook his head. Mr. Muscalini looked at us and continued. "I don't know much about making music. But I know teams. And a band is a team. The most talented team doesn't always win. Sometimes, it's all about the culture and togetherness. It's about bonding over the grind. It's about playing for the love of the game. Mayhem Mad Men has what it takes to win it all. But it's not about that. And it's not about you. It's about the fans. You have something to share with them. So share it!" Mr. Muscalini yelled while pumping his fist.

"I think we all appreciate the pep talk, but the band is already back together."

"I did it?" he questioned. "I did it!" Mr. Muscalini yelled, jumping in the air.

We all just laughed and let Mr. Muscalini have the victory.

"Well, we still need a guitarist," I said, looking over at Sophie across the way with Sammie. I looked at Luke. "I think you should do it."

"Let's do it together."

"Okay," I said.

Luke and I walked over to Sophie. She looked at us, confused.

"What's going on?" she asked.

"We've got a question to ask," I said.

"This can't be good," Sammie said.

Sophie ignored Sammie. "What is it?"

I looked at Luke and then back at Sophie. "Do you want to be the guitarist for Mayhem Mad Men? There's an opening."

"I heard that," she said, chuckling. "My answer is yes, on one condition."

"What is it?" Luke and I asked simultaneously.

"Nobody in the band tries to kiss me."

Luke nodded in agreement.

"What about me?" I asked. "I'm your boyfriend."

"I think I remember that," she said. "All members of the band, except my boyfriend."

Sammie giggled. Luke's eyes bulged. My face flushed redder than Clifford the Big Red Dog.

25

I t was crunch time. Battle of the Bands was upon us. We practiced and practiced every day leading up to the Battle. Even Luke did. We wanted to win. We wanted to beat Love Puddle. But really, we wanted to prove to ourselves that we were good enough and that we could have fun playing together. Leighton had given me so many pointers, I wasn't sure I could remember them all. Or any.

Battle of the Bands was about to begin. The stage was set in the infield of a minor league baseball stadium. There were thousands of people in the stands and hundreds more on the field in front of the stage. It was mayhem. And the Battle hadn't even begun.

Brody gave us the rundown of Battle of the Bands. He was the only one who had ever been there. I'm sure French Lisp embarrassed themselves there, but still, he had the experience.

"So, there are twenty bands in. Everybody plays one set and judges cut it to eight. Then it's tournament style, head to head. Win three head to heads and you're the Battle of the Bands champion!"

"Hey, looks like they're about to start," Just Charles said, pointing to the judges table and the announcers right next to them.

"Is that Calvin Conklin?" I asked, squinting to see who was sitting at the announcers table.

"Yep," Brody said. "He and Chelsea Wellesley are the hosts. They do it every year."

"He's such a doofus," I said.

"Yeah, and Chelsea hates him, too."

We walked closer to them to get a better view. Even from far away, you could see how perfectly crafted Calvin's hair was and his sparkly white teeth. Chelsea was like twenty-five years old with blond hair.

The speakers boomed with Calvin's voice, "Welcome, Battle fans! We are live on Channel Two, W-S.T.I.N.K. This is our twelfth annual Battle of the Bands contest. As you already know, I'm Calvin Conklin."

Chelsea looked at Calvin expectantly.

"Oh, and to my left is the glorious Chelsea Wellesly. Say that ten times fast, huh?"

"I bet you can't," she said.

Calvin took a deep breath. "Chelsea Wellesley, Chelsea Wellesley, Chelsea Wellesley, Chelsea Wellesley, Chelsea Wesley, Chelsea Chelsea, Kelsey Wiseley, Colonel Mosely, Colonel Moosey, Cloning Mooses." He took another deep breath. "Piece of cake."

"Yes, that was near perfect," Chelsea said with a smirk. "I'm glad I'm DVRing this."

"Well, let's get back to it, shall we?" Calvin asked. "It's a talented field of twenty bands. Leading the way are a few standouts. We have everyone's favorite, Goat Turd. But looking to squash Goat Turd is Thunder Toes, last year's runner up. Quiet Scream and Loud Hamster are set to pump up the volume while Sweet Booger's tunes just melt in your mouth."

"Excuse me while I vomit," Chelsea said to laughter.

"What am I forgetting Colonel, er, Chelsea?"

"Your Momma's a Liar," she said, simply.

Calvin's eyes bulged. "I know we've had our disagreements, but we've always kept it professional. Please leave my mother out of this."

"I was talking about the band," Chelsea said, shaking her head.

"Oh, right," he said. "I was kidding. Obviously."

"Obviously," Chelsea said to laughter, again.

"There are a few newcomers to the scene with plenty of talent."

Luke looked at the rest of us. "This is where we come in."

But we didn't.

"That's right, Calvin. Four new bands expecting to make their mark are Cold Sore, Gingivitis, The Pin Heads, and Love Puddle."

"That stinks," Luke said.

"Doesn't matter," Brody said. "The judges pick the winners. Not Calvin."

IT WAS time for our performance. We stood backstage with Brody and Mr. Muscalini. Sophie was the only one who didn't look like she was going to puke. Even Mr. Muscalini was looking a little green, but it could've been too many kale smoothies and not nerves.

Mr. Muscalini stepped forward. "We're exactly where we want to be. We're the underdogs. They don't think we can do it. But we can! Let's stay focused. Play your hearts out. Leave it all out there on the stage."

"You don't want us to clean up after?" Luke asked.

Mr. Muscalini shook his head and said, "It's a sports expression. Just do your best. That's all that matters. Now get out there and create some mayhem!"

Energy surged through my body. I was ready for the war. We ran out onto the stage to cheers.

Brody called after us, "And don't mess up!"

That was really helpful.

But then I felt like I was forgetting something. I looked back at Ben and I felt my heart in my throat. Ben was missing! Just kidding. I was going to put on his eye and ear protection, but then I remembered he didn't need it anymore. Max Mulvihill had cured him.

We set up and kicked it off with "Cafeteria Delirium." Everything was going great. Sophie was crushing it on the guitar, so much better than Sly ever could. My dance moves were serviceable, Luke hadn't tried to kiss anyone in the band, and Ben was crushing it on the drums. But just as we were about to hit Sophie's guitar solo, her amp cut out. The rest of us weren't playing, so even though her fingers were flying up and down the guitar, there was zero sound coming out of the speakers.

The crowd's cheering died down. Nobody knew what was going on. Just Charles, who was standing behind Sophie on stage, ran over to the amplifier, and plugged it back in. The music blared once again, catching us all by surprise. Sophie finished up the solo, the crowd cheering once again.

I sang, "Last week I got the runs! I got Cafeteria Delirium!" I forced a smile to the crowd.

The song ended to cheers, but I was fuming. We all were.

I walked back to Sophie, shaking my head. "This has Randy written all over it."

"Ya think?" Sophie yelled. Her face softened. "I'm sorry. It's not your fault. I didn't mean to yell at you."

As we came off the stage, frustrated, Mr. Muscalini gathered us. "You showed heart out there. Sometimes the calls go against us, but you kept fighting. Now all we can do is wait."

We knew there were a lot of good bands in the competition, but we didn't want to watch any of the performances. We didn't want to psych ourselves out if they were really good.

After all the bands were done, we returned to the crowd to hear the announcement on who would move forward. Calvin and Chelsea were running the show again.

"Before the battle can continue, it's time to chop the field down to size," Calvin said. "Are you ready?" he asked Chelsea.

"No, I'd just like to sit here doing nothing."

"Well, I, umm," Calvin stumbled, seemingly not sure of how to respond.

"Ok, I'm ready now. It's time for us to give you the top eight!" Chelsea waved an envelope to the cheering crowd.

"I see what you did there," Calvin said. "Can't get one past me."

"Never," Chelsea said, smirking. "There are some surprises here, right Calvin?"

"Nope. I pegged 'em all."

Chelsea rolled her eyes and started to open the envelope.

"Are you going to open it or should I?" Calvin said, reaching for the envelope.

Chelsea smacked his hand away and started to read, "The first band into the finals and our #1 seed is...The Pin Heads!"

The crowd went crazy. The Pin Heads hugged and then trotted up to the stage. I hoped to join them up there next. But nope. It was Cold Sore, Plumber's Crack, 64 Farts, Goat Turd, and Gingivitis next. There were two spots left and fourteen bands. You didn't have to be a math whiz like me to figure out the odds weren't good.

"All we need is one spot, gentlemen," Mr. Muscalini said, "And Gordo."

Ben smiled and said, "I am one with your jokes, sir."

Mr. Muscalini looked confused.

Until that point, I hadn't seen much of Randy, Sly, or the rest of Love Puddle, but my luck had run out. Love Puddle, being the rude punks that they are, pushed their way through the crowd, toward the stage.

A hard jab to my back seemed to pop my kidney. I grabbed my back, wincing in pain.

"Oh, pardon me," Randy said, over-the-top politely.

I was in too much pain to say anything. Randy kept walking while Sly and Nick laughed.

"Are you okay?" Sophie asked.

"Superb. I think I have two of whatever he just broke." Well, now one.

I shook it off and focused back on Calvin and Chelsea. Neither Love Puddle nor Mayhem Mad Men were in the finals. If one of us made it and the other one didn't, things at camp were gonna get ugly. And at school, for that matter. If we lost, Randy would be talking about it for years.

"Two spots left!" Calvin yelled.

"And the next band the judges sent to the finals is...Love Puddle!" Chelsea yelled. The crowd erupted into cheers.

My hope meter dropped from 'Cautiously optimistic' to 'We stink and we're not gonna make it' as Chelsea was set to deliver the death blow to twelve bands that were about to be cut from the competition.

Calvin tried to swipe the card from Chelsea, but she was way ahead of him. She tossed the card from one hand to the other and slapped his in the process.

"Oww! You didn't have to do that," Calvin said like a baby.

Chelsea ignored him. "The judges' final selection heading into the Battle of the Bands head to head is..."

The crowd's cheers fell to a hush. Some people shouted out the bands that they wanted to get in. My heart was racing a mile a minute. Sophie clung to my arm while Mr. Muscalini hid his eyes with his oversized hands.

The anticipation was about to end me. Chelsea teased us with the long wait, creating dramatic tension like a Hollywood movie writer. My heart was about to explode. And then Calvin grabbed the card, stuffed it in his mouth, and ate it.

26

Gotcha. Even Calvin isn't that much of an ego maniac. Randy, maybe. Calvin did try to grab the card again, but was unsuccessful. Chelsea dodged the swipe and stared at the card. She continued, "... Mayhem Mad Men!"

The crowd exploded into cheers. Our group, including Brody and Mr. Muscalini joined into a giant hug, screaming, and jumping around together in a circle. For a bunch of nerds, it was a pretty coordinated effort. We eventually made our way onto the stage with the other seven groups. Cameron Quinn from Goat Turd and Josh from Plumber's Crack gave me a chill head nod. I smiled back. I smiled even more when I saw Randy and Sly grumbling. The looks on their faces were priceless.

Because we were the last band in, we were up against the #1 seed: The Pin Heads. They were a college band that had been on the music scene for a while. Their singer was supposedly just as good as Cameron Quinn and their guitarist was one of the best around. We had an uphill battle ahead of us.

Calvin and Chelsea introduced the first battle. The crowd fell to a hush as the finals were about to kick off.

"Well, it's time for the true battle to begin!" Calvin yelled. The fans joined him.

"Any predictions for The Pin Heads versus Mayhem Mad Men?" Chelsea asked.

"Pin Heads, no question, Chelsea. Can't believe you're even asking. They are going to win the whole thing."

We were already backstage ready to play, so we heard every word Calvin spoke. I looked around at the band. You could see it on their faces. The excitement that we felt after getting into the finals was gone. The prospect of losing had made it into each of our heads, which was not what you wanted when you were about to play.

Mr. Muscalini reminded us, "He didn't think you would make it to the finals, either."

"Yeah, he's an idiot," I added.

"Remember when he thought Austin was a time traveler when he interviewed him at the science fair?" Sophie asked.

The band laughed and seemed to perk up a little.

"Just go out there, have fun, and do your best," Mr. Muscalini said.

We did just that. We let it rip. The crowd was starting to know the words. When we were rocking out on "Cafeteria Delirium", I heard a bunch of people of people join me by screaming, "Last week I got the runs!" It was crazy to hear them sing along with me on a song I wrote, especially a song that included getting diarrhea after eating bad seafood.

We left the stage to cheers. We were all pretty pleased with how it went. There were a few mistakes, but none that were terrible and most people probably didn't even notice them. Not like falling off the stage or sending an old lady to the hospital.

～

WE DIDN'T WATCH the Pin Heads, but based on the cheers we heard, it sounded like they did pretty well, although Brody said things got a little weird at the end when the lead guitarist got a little too crazy with a solo and smashed his guitar like a lunatic. The crowd loved it, but he said the judges didn't look too excited. So, we had a shot.

After their performance, we headed up to the stage for the announcement of the winner. Sophie and I held hands as we waited for Calvin and Chelsea to reveal the judges' decision. Luke was on the other side of Sophie, so I kept checking to make sure he didn't try to hold her hand or anything.

A judge made his way to the hosts' table. He was older than any of the participants, but he looked like he wasn't too far from competing in Battle of the Bands himself. He handed the envelope to Chelsea. She grabbed it and pulled it away from Calvin's swipe, and shook her head.

Chelsea opened the envelope, smiled, and said, "Mayhem Mad Men! Wow! What a shocker!"

Our crew went nuts, jumping up and down. Sophie and I hugged. Luke joined in, which I wasn't overly thrilled about, but I let it slide.

"Holy guacamole!" Calvin yelled. "I can't believe I called that one!"

Chelsea muttered, "What an idiot."

She wasn't wrong.

"Next up, we have Cold Sore versus Plumber's Crack. What do you think, Calvin?"

"My sixth sense is telling me Cold Sore. And it's never wrong. Cold Sore all the way."

"Yep, I'm sure you're right. As always," she said, smirking to the crowd.

Both groups performed and the judges' pick was in. Chelsea held the envelope in her hand.

"Can I open it this time? Please?" Calvin begged.

"Okay, just this once." Chelsea dangled the envelope in front of Calvin. He looked like a dog about to get a treat.

Calvin reached for it. Chelsea pulled it away with a laugh. "Maybe next time." She tore open the envelope as Calvin pouted, and said, "Looks like the judges love Plumber's Crack!"

Calvin's pout disappeared as he threw his hands in the air. "My win streak continues!"

The competition continued. Chelsea said, "Next up, we have Love Puddle versus 64 Farts. Is it 64 or 65 Farts?"

Calvin scoffed. "That's such a dumb question. 64. 65 Farts would be ridiculous."

Chelsea shook her head. "Right..." She looked over at Calvin. "What's your sixth sense telling you on this one?" Chelsea asked, nearly laughing.

"Chelsea, I'm not a hater of Love Puddle by any means, but I just love how the Farts sound."

Chelsea muttered, "I bet you do."

Both Love Puddle and 64 Farts put on great performances. It could've gone either way. I hoped 64 Farts would knock off Randy and Love Puddle.

Calvin looked at Chelsea and said, "I think it's my turn to announce the next winner, right?"

"It's in my contract. Maybe next year."

"That hurts me deeply," Calvin said.

"I didn't think there was anything deep about you," Chelsea countered, as she grabbed the envelope from the judge.

The crowd started to chant, "Farts, Farts, Farts, Farts!"

"Well, the crowd is making their choice. They've said 'Farts' so many times I lost count, but with their dedicated fans, I'm pretty sure they'll stop at 64," Calvin said, and then chuckled at Chelsea. "65. So ridiculous."

Chelsea ignored him as she opened the envelope. "Another upset! It's Love Puddle!"

My heart sank. Most of our band groaned.

Calving yelled into the mic, "This is getting unbelievable! I hit another one right on the money! Even I'm almost amazed at how amazing I am!"

Chelsea forced a smile and said, "We're astonished. Who's your pick for our next battle, Goat Turd versus Gingivitis?"

"Gingivitis is gonna take this one."

After the performances, Chelsea announced the winner.

"And what do you know? It's Goat Turd! You missed every single one," Chelsea said, laughing at Calvin.

"What competition are you watching?"

27

And then it was down to four: Plumber's Crack versus your favorite band, Mayhem Mad Men and the unlovable Love Puddle versus Goat Turd. I couldn't believe we had made it that far after where we had started from earlier in the summer, and the fact that we had broken up and lost our guitarist only a week ago.

My nervousness was growing. I wasn't sure if I could improve every performance to keep winning. We needed two more wins and we would be Battle of the Bands champion. I almost couldn't believe we were that close. But so was Randy. And that meant Randy would be dipping into his bag of tricks with both hands. And maybe even his feet. You never knew with that one.

It put us all on edge. It's like walking into a room, not sure if you'll get slapped in the face, kicked in your privates, tripped, or splashed with a bucket of pee. Yep, it was that bad.

Our performance started off strong. "Gym Class Zero" had the women in tears and "Middle School Mayhem" had everyone rocking out. By the time we were halfway through

"Cafeteria Delirium", the crowd was in a frenzy. I stood near the front of the stage, singing about nearly puking up all the food my school serves.

The crowd chanted, "Jump! Jump! Jump!"

I thought about it for a minute, but I was too nervous. I wasn't ready to attempt another crowd surf. Visions of old lady dentures in my mouth rattled around in my brain.

It was a good thing, too. Well, sort of. As I stepped toward the crowd, my foot slipped from something wet on the stage. If I had hit it running, I probably would've killed an old lady. Still, it wasn't good. My foot shot out in front of me, catching me by surprise. The crowd roared. I think they thought I meant to do a Kung-Fu kick or something. And then things went awry. I caught my balance and continued on with "Gym Class Zero", which was nearing the end. As I attempted to dance my way across the stage, a giant mass of liquid flew through the air from the crowd.

I had no time to react or see who threw it. The bulk of the water hit me square in the face. I lost my footing as I tried to dodge the attack. I stumbled onto a puddle (interesting choice of words, I know), and slip slided across the stage. The mic shorted out, so we couldn't finish with our beloved ending: 'You a hero? Nah, man. I'm a gym class zero.' I continued to slide across the stage like a surfer. That didn't want to be surfing. That didn't know how to surf. And was heading straight for a drum set.

I let out a blood-curdling scream, which I hoped no one heard, as I surfed past Sophie, Luke, and Just Charles, none of whom knew what to do, or just wanted to see me smash into the drum set. Ben caught sight of me at the last second, but it was too late for him to get out of the way as I smashed into the drums, tumbling over them, and into him, taking both of us to the ground in a heap.

After I regained my senses, I whisper-groaned, "I, too, am one with the drums."

∽

WE WERE NERVOUS AND ANGRY. We knew it was Love Puddle. We stood backstage, pacing and waiting for Brody to return from his pow wow with the judges.

He walked toward us, all smiles and gave us a thumbs up.

"What's the deal?" Luke asked.

"Judges said they won't hold the crash/finale to our song against us."

We all exhaled at the same time, nearly knocking Brody down.

Sophie asked what we all were thinking, "What about Love Puddle?"

Brody's smile disappeared. "No evidence. They deny the whole thing."

Mr. Muscalini rushed up. "Better head out to the stage! They're announcing the winner of your round!"

We hustled out to the stage, staring at Plumber's Crack. The audience looked as anxious as we were.

Calvin's voice boomed from the loud speakers, "What a day! It's a real battle!"

Chelsea shook her head. "You'd think it was named that or something." Chelsea opened the envelope. "I believe your pick was Plumber's Crack. And wrong you are! It's Mayhem Mad Men!"

"What?" I yelled. I couldn't believe it. And then joined it our celebratory jumping hug again as the crowd chanted, "Mad Men! Mad Men! Mad Men!"

Chelsea spoke into the mic, "Last battle before the championship performance! It's Goat Turd versus Love Puddle. What's the prediction? You have to get one right, no?"

Calvin laughed. "Such a jokester. I'm going with Love Puddle. No, Goat Turd!"

Chelsea looked over at the judges and said, "Should they still play? Love Puddle's gonna win."

She was right. After amazing performances from both bands, Chelsea announced, Love Puddle, as the winner.

Chelsea looked at Calvin and asked, "You sure you're not a weatherman?"

"God knows I have the looks, but no," Calvin said to Chelsea and then to the crowd, "Here we are, the final two! Love Puddle versus Mayhem Mad Men! I knew it all along. Which one of these up-and-coming bands will make its mark in Battle of the Bands history?"

"Whichever one you don't pick to win," Chelsea said.

"Well, I'm just gonna keep this one to myself. I'm tired of your judgement," he said like a whiny baby. A whiny baby that can talk and understands the pain involved in judgement.

Love Puddle went first. Judging from the crowd's reaction, they must've played a great set. We tried not to let it get to us, but I'm not sure I did a good job of that.

I paced around in a circle, going over some dance moves in my head, nerves shooting through my body from head to toe. The rest of the band wasn't doing much better. Sophie bit her nails while messing around on her phone while Luke and Just Charles were busy worrying about how Love Puddle would attempt to sabotage our performance. Even Mr. Muscalini wasn't himself. He was quiet for a change.

"They could cut the power," Luke said.

"Collapse the stage maybe," Just Charles said. "Whatever it is, I'm nervous."

Ben stood up calmly. "There is nothing to worry about. The universe is aligning for our victory as we speak. Love Puddle won't do anything to sabotage us."

"Who is he?" Luke asked me.

I shook my head and shrugged with a smile.

Mr. Muscalini stood up and said, "Nothing to fear, gents, and Ms. Rodriguez." He took a few steps toward Love Puddle in the distance, put two fingers in his mouth and whistled. You know, one of those slimy, I don't-know-how-they-do-it whistles. Randy looked over at Mr. Muscalini.

Mr. Muscalini summoned Randy with a simply finger curl. Randy nodded and started walking toward us. Mr. Muscalini turned back to us, looking at the underside of his pointer finger. "You think I need to work this out?" he asked, squeezing the meat on it.

"I think you're good, sir," I said.

Randy stopped in front of Mr. Muscalini. He put on his best fake smile. "You wanted to see me, sir?"

"Mister Warblemacher," Mr. Muscalini said, "No more funny business. This better be a fair fight. I can't have a cheater as the captain of my football team."

Randy gulped. "Yes, sir," he said.

"Now, run along. And good luck," Mr. Muscalini said.

Randy nodded sheepishly, turned, and walked away.

Ben looked at us and smiled, "See? The stars are aligning."

Luke looked up into the blue sky. "Huh?"

Sophie and I just looked at each other and laughed.

"It's time," Ben said.

"Already?" Just Charles said.

"They're ready early," Ben said.

Brody walked around the corner and yelled, "Let's go! They're ready early. We kick off in five minutes!"

Ben winked at me and said, "Time to express some badditude."

We walked out onto the stage to cheers. Ben kicked off our final performance of Battle of the Bands with a "Mayhem Mad Men!"

I pulled the mic out of the stand and sang, "6 A.M. wakeup. The halls are filled with too much body spray, perfume and makeup. Gotta claw through the fumes just to get to the bathroom. History's a mystery. Foreign language is pure misery."

The crowd was loving it. I got a little too crazy and threw out a Kung-Fu kick. I snapped it out like a master. The crowd roared.

I continued singing, "Algebra and training bras. I just found a band aid in my coleslaw. Field trips to landfills and fire drills. Study hall, dodge ball, why can't we just chill?

Middle School Mayhem! Parents think we're learning, don't know what to say to them."

I spun around and got a little dizzy, but made my way over to Sophie, who jammed like a superstar on the guitar. I knew she had a great voice from our time in music class, as well as when she was a lead in the school musical. I held the microphone out for both of us to sing.

She joined me, smiling. "Things have never been so clear, you gotta get me outta here, I'm so filled with fear, who came up with this idea? Middle School Mayhem, another date with detention, I'm goin' on the run, Middle School Mayhem."

I looked over at Luke, who was focused on the bass, laying down the rhythm like a boss. I took a few steps toward him and nodded expectantly.

His eyes widened and then he nodded back.

I held out the mic as Luke and I sang, "School dances, three-day-old romances, can't believe we broke up. Dudes are so afraid of girls, can't even say, what's up? Somebody farted, was it you?" I pointed to him and he smirked. "Did you see the lunch menu? Ugh, another day of radioactive beef stew."

I headed back to the front of the stage. I needed to work the crowd. I was going to go for it. What, you ask? You'll just have to wait and see.

I gave a few high-fives without falling. Ben must've been right about it all working out. I sang, "Nobody knows what's in those Sloppy Joes! This whole place is a sham, if I could just find fame on Instagram. Middle School Mayhem. Parent's think we're learning, but they don't gotta clue. The principal is cray cray, we need to start a coup."

And then it was time to unleash the badditude. I had tried it once before and it resulted in getting tomatoed off the stage. I hoped it would work this time. I yelled into the mic and pointed to the crowd, "You know the words! Everybody sing!"

I held the mic out as the entire crowd, except for Love Puddle, bellowed, "Things have never been so clear, you gotta get me outta here, I'm so filled with fear. Who came up with this idea? Middle School Mayhem, another date with detention, I'm goin' on the run, Middle School Mayhem."

I yelled into the microphone, "Are you ready?"

The crowd threw their hands up and cheered. I took a running start, jumped off the edge of the stage, and soared like an eagle above the first few rows of the crowd. I closed my eyes, hoping to God that the old lady with the dentures was not the only one who would try to catch me this time.

I hit my peak in the air, rolled to my back like I learned from Cameron Quinn, and started to fall. I fell a little longer than I thought I should. Maybe it was the protein shakes Mr. Muscalini had me drinking that gave me extra height. Or I was about to humiliate myself and send some poor old lady to the hospital.

And then it happened. I felt the glorious cushion of dozens of hands and heard the roar of the crowd. The crowd passed me from one side of the stage to the other as Ben unleashed a monster drum solo. With a smile on his face! The crowd went nuts.

The crowd threw me up on the stage (not in a gross way). I ran across the front of the stage and slid on my knees as I sang, "Middle School Mayhem!" as Brody unleashed the Sparkulars and Ben smashed the symbol at the end of his solo.

I looked out at the crowd. It was literally mayhem. I didn't get a great look because the rest of the Mad Men, including Brody and Mr. Muscalini rushed and then crushed me. We ended up in a giant pile. From the force of it all, Sophie's face connected with mine. Her lips brushed mine ever so slightly. Was it a kiss? I wasn't sure.

Sophie and I stared at each other in silence only inches away.

She broke the silence, "Hey,"

"Hey," I said. I literally couldn't think of anything else to say.

"I'm not wearing an old lady's dentures, am I?" Sophie asked.

I laughed. "No. And she was a better kisser than you."

Sophie feigned anger. "That wasn't real, dummy."

And then I felt like a dummy when I realized the rest of the band had gotten up while Sophie and I remained on the stage floor. We got up to cheers from the audience. My face flushed red, yet again.

LOVE PUDDLE FOLLOWED our amazing performance with one of their own. Randy was on fire. Literally. And not like Mayhem Mad Men in our earlier days when we accidentally set the stage and Ben on fire. It was part of their performance. During their song, Burning Love, Randy danced across the stage into the grand finale. As he fell to his knees with his back to the crowd during the final note, a flame ignited on the back of his shirt, lighting not a fart, but the shape of a heart. The girls went wild. Some were even crying. I think it was just because they were scared of the fire. The spotlights cut out, leaving only the view of the burning heart on stage.

"Wow! That was amazing!" Calvin yelled into his microphone. "I totally called that Randy Warblemacher would set himself on fire!"

"No, you didn't," Chelsea said. "But those were the two best performances of the night, by far. Some of the best we've ever seen in this contest!"

Calvin added, "It's a three-person judge panel. And they're gonna have their hands full tonight!"

We joined Love Puddle on the stage as far away from them as possible. I was afraid I might fall off the stage. And there were no old ladies to break my fall.

A woman judge walked over to Calvin and Chelsea. She held out the envelope in front of Chelsea. Calvin dove from his chair and snagged the envelope. Chelsea got her hands on it, too. They struggled for it. The judge froze, her face aghast. It kind of reminded me of Ben back in the day. I took a deep breath. We were seconds away from the winner being announced.

Well, a few seconds turned into a few minutes. The battle for the envelope was almost as exciting as the Battle of the Bands. Calvin got his hand on the envelope. Chelsea turned her back to him as he maintained a death grip on the envelope, his arm over her shoulder. She used it to her advantage. Chelsea stood up with force and then dropped to one knee, tossing Calvin over her shoulder. He landed on his back with a whimper. He rolled over onto his stomach with a groan.

Even though Calvin was defeated, Chelsea wasn't finished. She sat on Calvin's back, slipped both her hands underneath his chin, and screamed, "I hate you!" before executing the devastating and ego-crushing Camel Clutch. Calvin's eyes bulged like they were about to pop from his sockets.

Security rushed the feuding hosts. It took three hulking guards to rip Chelsea's grip apart. They dragged her off, kicking and screaming.

Mr. Muscalini broke our stunned silence, "How much do you think she weigh?"

Sophie said, "What? Why?"

"The wrestling team needs someone in the 104-pound weight class. Kieran Murphy is terrible."

"Sir, I don't think she's in middle school," I said.

'Right. Disappointing."

After Calvin regrouped, he sat back down to a few boos and some cheers. The envelope sat in front of him atop the table in fourteen shredded pieces. He tried to piece them together for a moment unsuccessfully until the judge came over and whispered in his ear.

Calvin nodded to himself and then addressed the rest of us. His tone of voice was different. It was serious. Humble even. He said, "There are moments in life when you need to rise about the challenges that life presents you. One can only hope that you are prepared for them. Or that security is there to bail you out if you're not." The crowd laughed.

Calvin continued, "Tonight, we had twenty amazing bands put their heart and souls into entertaining us all. Let us honor them now." The crowd cheered. "Now we're down to two. Two underdogs that I myself thought talented, but nowhere near likely to take home the Championship of Battle of the Bands. Before we announce tonight's winner, please show your respect and admiration for Love Puddle and Mayhem Mad Men!" The crowd cheered again.

Our band stood side by side across our side of the stage, arm in arm.

A chant broke out in the crowd, "Love Puddle! Love Puddle!"

And then a second one in response. "Mad Men! Mad Men!" Ours was louder, in case you were wondering.

"And now, the moment you've all been waiting for," Calvin said with a seemingly genuine smile. "I give you your champion of this year's Battle of the Bands..." Calvin paused for a moment and then my heart imploded when I heard the first word out of this mouth, "Luhhh, it's Mayhem Mad Men!"

The crowd erupted into a roar of approval. I didn't know what to do. It took a minute to even register. I thought Love Puddle was going to win. The band engulfed me in hugs.

"We did it!" I yelled.

The celebration felt like a dream. I had never been so happy in my life. Sophie, Ben, and Luke all wrapped their arms around me.

"We're not nerds anymore!" Luke yelled.

"I thought it was about the fun?" Ben asked.

"It was, but still, we're not nerds!"

As the crowd died down, there were just a few official-looking people around, Love Puddle, and our crew, cleaning up our equipment.

Mr. Muscalini gathered us up. "I've never been more proud of a team than I am today. I don't care that we won. I care that we persevered. I care that when the game was on the line, you all stepped up and gave your best. And the person who led us through that, besides me, of course, was our M.V.P. Bring it in here, Gordo!" Mr. Muscalini held his hulking arms out wide. "I've got a special, bone-crushing hug just for you!"

Ben stepped forward reluctantly. The rest of us cheered him on.

"Way to go, Gordo!" Luke said.

I started chanting, "M.V.P.! M.V.P.!"

Mr. Muscalini wrapped his arms around Ben and squeezed. Ben's head looked like it might pop up, but thankfully it stayed connected.

I was distracted when I thought I saw Sly out of the corner of my eye. I looked over to see him being pulled by his ear by someone I can only assume was his mother.

"Sylvester Wentworth Flurf, you will come with me right this instant!" the woman yelled.

"His name is Sylvester Flurf?" I said, almost laughing too hard to get the words out.

"Wentworth?" Sophie asked.

"No wonder he pretended he was too cool to need a last name," I said.

And then Randy walked up to us, his head held a little high for somebody who had just gotten crushed, and wearing sunglasses after the sun was barely still afloat. Does the sun float? I mean, how does it stay up there? I needed to do some research.

Anyway, Randy stopped in front of me, pulled off his sunglasses super cool like an airplane pilot, and stared at me with a raised eyebrow.

"What are you looking at, Davenfart?"

"You stopped in front of me."

"You have something you want to say to me?" Randy asked.

"Umm, no. Again, you stopped in front of me. Is there something you want to say to me?" I asked, uncertain of what was going on.

Randy stepped closer to me and whispered, "The competition might be over, but you and me aren't done, Davenfart. Not by a long shot."

"Why are you whispering?"

"Raising the tension."

"Shouldn't you be yelling then?"

"You want me to yell at you?"

"Not really. Are we done here? I have some celebrating to do. Maybe you don't know, but my band just won Battle of the Bands." I couldn't help myself.

"Not just yet, Davenfart. You might've gotten lucky and swayed the opinions of a few tone-deaf judges, but you haven't won anything. You think sixth grade was tough for you? Just wait until next year."

I had nothing more to say to him. I turned my back on Randy and walked over to the rest of the group.

Randy called after me, "This ain't over, Davenfart."

I ignored him and looked at the crew. "Bring it in," I said, solemnly. "I have bad news."

Everyone stepped toward me, concern across their faces. They probably thought I was going to say something revengeful about Randy, but I was over him.

I continued, "If Sophie is going to stay in the band, and I think we all want that, unfortunately, I don't think we can be the Mayhem Mad Men."

The group groaned in disgust and disappointment.

And then Luke's face lit up as he called out enthusiastically, "I have an idea!"

I just looked at him and said, "Don't you dare!"

WANT FREE STUFF?

ACTIVITY SHEETS?

SHORT STORIES?

DISCOUNTED BOOKS?

OTHER BONUSES?

C.T.'S MONTHLY
NEWSLETTER

OF COURSE, YOU DO!

ctwalsh.fun/msm4bonuses

BOOK 5 PREVIEW CHAPTER
MIDDLE SCHOOL MAYHEM: MEDIEVAL MAYHEM

Behold, noble subjects. It is I, Sir Austin Davenport the Hilarious. The tale I shall tell this day with my most mysterious of voices brings us back to medieval times. It is a tale of betrayal, courage in the face of impossible odds, blood-curdling hatred, enduring love, horrifying sights like my principal in tights, and triumph over evil and nightmares, mainly of my principal in tights.

The tale begins in the dark ages. No, not medieval times. Middle school. The first day of seventh grade, to be exact. We started right where we left off. War. No, I'm not being dramatic.

My best friend, Ben, and I walked in the creaky double doors and soaked in all the gloriousness of Cherry Avenue Middle School, which was basically just my girlfriend, Sophie, who I spotted across the atrium. A smile spread across my face as I walked toward her.

"This year is going to be so much better," Ben said, cheerfully.

"Really? Why?" I asked.

Before Ben could answer, I heard the whiny voice of the

Dark Lord, Principal Buthaire, behind me. "Mister Davenport, I dreamt of this moment all summer." Feel free to call him, The Prince of Buttness, if you prefer.

I turned around to see the only one of my three nemeses that had a mustache (as much as my brother, Derek, tried to grow one) standing before me. Ben scurried off without a word. I didn't blame him, although witnesses were always preferred when I was dealing with Principal Buthaire or Randy Warblemacher, my most hated nemesis.

I was confused. "What moment is that, sir?"

"The one where you and I meet exactly as I planned," Principal Buthaire said and then followed it with an evil cackle.

It was too early in the morning for evil cackles. "That's kinda weird, sir."

Principal Buthaire ignored me. "We may have tied last year, but I'm going to win this year. Bigly."

He was lying. We didn't tie last year. I won. Bigly. He did make my first year of middle school less than enjoyable, but I bested him in every head to head battle.

The Dark Lord continued, "You walk around here like you're Prince Gopher or something, and that ends now." He took a deep breath, seemingly about to continue.

I interrupted, "Is that a real person?" I knew our mascot was a gopher, but I was pretty certain there was no prince attached to the story. I wasn't even sure if there were any gophers in our entire county.

"I don't know," Principal Butt Hair (he claims it's pronounced Boo-tare, but look at the spelling) said, annoyed. "Ask Dr. Dinkledorf. He's the historian. Where was I?"

"You were berating me for no reason, sir."

"Ah, yes. Thank you. You're not middle school royalty no matter how much you parade around here like you are."

I learned enough last year to know that arguing didn't make a difference, so I just kept my mouth shut, which was not always easy for me.

"You may have won Battle of the Bands over the summer, but you will rue the day, rue the day, I say, that you challenged me! I'm the Emperor and you will fall in line or you will find yourself in the dungeon of detention. Consider yourself warned, Mister Davenport," he said in as deep a voice as he could.

"Noted, sir," I said, taking a step back as we were almost nose to nose as I looked up at him. And a note to self: 7th grade was not going to be better than last year. I would make sure to inform my foolish best friend that his optimism was not warranted.

I saluted him and turned on my heels, eager to get as far away from that lunatic as possible. I headed over toward Sophie, Ditzy Dayna, Ben, and Just Charles.

"Hey," I greeted them all. Sophie and Ditzy Dayna gave me hugs. I wasn't sure Dayna remembered me. She was not exactly the sharpest knife in the drawer.

"Oh, my God!" Sophie yelled excitedly as she looked at the swarm of students pass by.

"What?" I asked. I thought somebody famous was in the building.

"They're so cute. The sixth graders are so tiny."

Ditzy Dayna added in baby talk, "They're wike wittle babies. I just want to pinch their cheeks."

The rest of us laughed.

"We were them last year," Ben said. And then his face went white. "Oh, my Gopher! No. Just no." Ben was looking past us down the hall.

"Dude, are you okay? What did you see?" I thought Ben might faint. And then I saw her. Or it. Technically, she was a girl, but all we saw was a monster walking toward us.

Sophie whisper yelled, "Regan Storm!"

She was the most unlikable of people. She was at Randy Warblemacher level. If you haven't heard about him yet, don't worry. You will. But what was Regan doing at Cherry Avenue? We met her at camp over the summer, but she wasn't in our school the year prior and Sophie had said she was from Bear Creek, which was a different school district.

If anybody was parading around like royalty, it was Regan. But I doubted that Principal Buthaire would ever call her out on it. He gravitated toward idiots like her, my brother, and Randy. Like attracts like, as they say.

Regan walked down the hall announcing herself, "Make way for Regan Storm." She took a menacing step toward a small pack of sixth graders, who all scattered like bugs. Regan threw her head back and laughed.

"What the heck is she doing here?" Ben asked.

"She never said she was moving here when we were at camp," Sophie added.

"Maybe she won't be in any of our classes," I said, hopefully.

"Maybe she got on the wrong bus," Ditzy Dayna said, twirling her hair.

"To the wrong school district?" Ben asked, shaking his head.

Regan spotted us and stopped in front of us, her smirk nearly blocking the hallway. Ben took two steps back.

Regan stared at Sophie. "Morning, ladies."

I wasn't sure if she was referring to Ben, Just Charles, and me as ladies or not, but I wasn't about to ask and put myself in her crosshairs.

Sophie nodded and said monotone, "What's up?"

"You seem to be the It girl here, so just wanted to give you a heads up. There's a new queen in town."

Regan gave Sophie a pat on her cheek, smirked, and walked away.

❧

My first day of seventh grade was not going overly well as you already know. History with Dr. Dinkledorf continued that trend. I liked history well enough. And Dr. Dinkledorf was pretty cool for an old dude. He was definitely in my corner in my battle against Principal Buthaire, going so far as to encourage me to break some rules in order to stand up to the oppressive reign of Prince Butt Hair, one of my other pet nicknames for our esteemed principal.

I knew Ben was going to be in our class, so I figured it would be okay. I got to talking with Steven Miley while I waited for Ben to show up. Steven was a good dude, halfway between the nerd and athletic worlds, and nice.

"What'd you do this summer?" Steven asked as we sat at our desks, waiting for the bell to ring.

"My band, Mayhem Mad Men, won Battle of the Bands. What about you?"

"Oh, I played video games. I won Dawn of the Savages. So, about the same as yours."

I couldn't believe he was equating winning a video game to taking down great bands like Goat Turd and 64 Farts, and of course, Randy Warblemacher's own Love Puddle.

Before I could point out how much more awesome winning Battle of the Bands in real life was to pressing a button to shoot arrows at Neanderthals, history changed forever. Well, not like the history of the world. I was talking more like our history class.

Regan Storm and Randy Warblemacher walked in one after the other.

"Davenfart! I missed your stench!" Randy called out loud enough for the entire class to hear. A bunch of idiots laughed.

Ugh. "Glad to see you're still an immature turd licker, Warblemonster," I said. I got more laughter than he did. I track it on a spreadsheet.

Ben walked in, saw Randy and Regan, and nearly deflated like a fizzled balloon that you accidentally let go before it's tied. The good news was that he didn't make any high-pitched farting sounds, which was a plus.

Ben slipped into the seat next to me, shock still on his face. "We have to endure a whole year of history with not one, but two of those idiots?"

"Seems to be the case," I said, shrugging.

Dr. Dinkledorf stood in front of the class and cleared his throat. "Settle in class. For those of you who don't know me, my name is Dr. Dinkledorf."

"Dinkledork is more like it," Regan whispered.

Dr. Dinkledorf was probably the oldest teacher in the school, so his hearing was a bit less than perfect. He continued on as if he didn't hear Regan's insult, which he probably didn't. "It's going to be a wonderful year. We will begin studying the later medieval period with a specific focus on the Renaissance, one of my favorite topics to explore."

"Snore fest," Randy said.

"And this year, we have a special treat for our seventh graders. A field trip to the medieval town of Chester as it prepares for the 25th anniversary of the Jefferson County Renaissance fair!"

A few small claps echoed through the class room.

Dr. Dinkledorf looked at me with a wide smile. I gave him a thumbs up.

Randy looked over at me and mouthed, "Dork."

Dr. Dinkledorf said, "Permission slips are due by the end of the week."

Thankfully, I had third period with Sophie, Ben, and Sammie, and no Randy or Regan. I sat with them at lunch. There's nothing like school lunch at ten o'clock in the morning. And it looked like they started the year off with a bang. Ham loaf. Don't know what ham loaf is? You might not want to. But I'll tell you just in case. It's meat loaf, but with ham.

Look, nobody's expecting lobster thermidor for three dollars, but ham loaf on the first day? It was like they didn't care enough to even pretend it was going to be a good year. Everybody knows that most parents only ask about how school went on the first day. You tell them it went great because you have no homework and they served pizza and everybody's happy. But no, they couldn't even give us that.

I ate a bunch of corn as we chatted. Sammie was going on and on about cheerleading tryouts, which was kind of boring, so I just wondered what the point was of even eating corn when it comes out looking exactly like it did on the way in.

"I'm so nervous," Sammie said, playing with her food.

"Is that why you're not eating the ham loaf?" Ben asked with a smile.

That's why he's my best friend.

"Sophie," Sammie said, "I still can't believe you don't want to be a cheerleader. I wish you would've tried out with me."

Sophie shrugged. "It's not my thing. Hopefully, you and Dayna will make the team together."

I couldn't imagine Ditzy Dayna remembering any of the cheers, but I didn't want to dash any of Sammie's hopes.

"We find out today after school. Tryouts were two weeks! I learned so much. I can't wait."

The final bell rang throughout the school. Kids cheered like we had just survived a 12-round boxing match with the heavyweight champ. I'm not a boxing fan, but I'm pretty certain whoever the heavyweight champ was couldn't handle a day of middle school. I gathered my books and backpack at my locker. I heard footsteps stomping behind me.

"You're never gonna believe this!" Sammie said, annoyed.

"What?" I asked. I had a feeling she was going to tell me even if I didn't want to know.

"Regan Storm made the team! She didn't even try out!"

"She probably beat up your coach or pushed her into the pool or something." Maybe I was just bitter. She pushed Ben and me into the pool at summer camp. She totally caught me by surprise and I'm certain that she works out with a trainer. "Do you know how you did?"

"Oh, yeah. I made the team," she said, nonchalantly.

"Great! Just be happy that you made it. I'm happy for you."

"It is so exciting," she said, jumping up and down. She

didn't have any pom poms, but she was already looking the part of a cheerleader.

"Don't forget that we've been friends for basically our whole lives. Now that you're really cool, I'm just worried you're going to forget about me. Or worse."

Sammie pushed me, playfully. "Don't worry, dummy. Cheerleaders and dweebs can be friends."

"See? It's starting already," I said with raised eyebrows.

"I'm just kidding," Sammie said.

I hoped so, but I had seen it before. When nerds and other non-popular kids get accepted into the popular group, a lot of them change.

It was the first football game of the season, so the whole world stopped so we could worship the royalty of smelly kids with anger issues running in strange patterns across some finely-cut grass. Or maybe I just don't get it.

Perhaps you noticed. I don't really care about football. Sometimes, the strategy of it all was cool, but overall, I wasn't impressed. My dad always tried to get me to understand it. He loved football and watching Derek play it well. My mom was more the intellectual like me and didn't really know what was going on. Either Derek ran far with the ball, which was good, or he didn't run far with it, which was bad.

I sat in the stands with my parents and Sophie. The game was tied late in the fourth quarter and the fearsome Gophers had the ball against the Brighton Bisons.

My dad leaned over to me and Sophie and said, "Mr. Muscalini loves the 44 Blast. He's gonna call it once we get closer."

"What the heck is the 44 Blast?" I asked.

"It's a running play where the fullback leads the way, blasting through the line, opening a hole for the running back."

I understood what he was talking about, but I also found it kind of boring, so I imagined that instead the fullback blasted a worm hole into the core of the universe that Derek ran into and disappeared from, en route to another galaxy. What? Just some brotherly love.

"Got that?" I asked Sophie.

"Yep, Nick is gonna punch a hole in the line. Randy will hand off to Derek, who will follow Nick."

"She's a keeper," my dad said.

Sophie understood it more than I did. I smiled. "She is, but not because of her football knowledge."

Sophie and I both blushed. I rarely saw her embarrassed. I was usually embarrassing myself enough for the both of us.

The Gophers lined up against the Bisons, threatening to score from about ten yards out of the end zone. Randy stood behind center as the quarterback with Derek behind him as the running back and the gargantuan Nick DeRozan next to Derek as the fullback.

"Here it comes," my dad said, "44 Blast."

"If you know it's coming, don't they know it's coming?" That's at least something I could get my brain around. It's called game theory. It's super interesting. It analyzes competitive situations where the outcome of one player/participant is dependent on the choices of others. Sorry for the nerd diversion.

My dad answered, "Maybe, but with Nick blasting the hole and your brother's speed, it probably doesn't matter."

I secretly hoped that Brighton did know it was coming and rooted for Randy to get run over by a herd of Bison. Derek getting run over would be a close second on my wish list. You may find that a bit harsh, but Randy deserved a few herds worth of a trampling, and my brother at least a few stomps.

The team broke from the huddle and lined up in front of the Bisons. Randy yelled out, "Gopher 22! I wear pink underwear! I'm a dummy and can't ride a bike!" At least that's what it sounded like with his mouthpiece in.

Randy received the ball from the monster in front of him and turned to Nick DeRozan. He faked a handoff to Nick, who was lumbering to the hoard of clashing Neanderthals. Nick blasted two incoming Bison like he was swatting flies, as Randy handed the ball to Derek, who followed a few steps behind Nick. Dudes were flying everywhere like pins in a bowling alley. Derek ran untouched, spun around a defender and into the end zone for a touchdown.

The crowd went nuts. My parents jumped up, cheering. My dad looked down at me and lightly slapped my shoulder. "See? 44 Blast gets it done every time."

I clapped a few times just so nobody thought I was too weird. It was like if you didn't like football, you had something wrong with you.

Derek ran to the sideline holding the football over his head as his teammates mobbed him. He broke free from the crowd as he passed by the bouncing cheerleaders and flipped the ball to Sammie, who was shaking her pom poms wildly. She stopped dead in her tracks, frozen. The ball hit her in the head and bounced across the ground. Regan stood next to her and laughed. Sammie's brain unfroze and when she realized what had just happened, she thrust her pom poms in the air and kicked her leg exuberantly, her shin touching her shoulder, and unfortunately (or fortunately, depending on how you look at it) kicked Regan in the face. Regan fell to the floor, holding her nose. I couldn't wait to thank Sammie for that.

The 44 Blast, which resulted in Derek's touchdown, was the difference in the game. The mighty Gophers stomped the Bisons 21-14. And everybody was running around like world hunger had been solved because a bunch of middle schoolers ran across a line three times holding an oddly-shaped ball.

After the game, we hung out in the atrium of the school. We waited for Mr. Muscalini to give a motivational speech or whatever he does after games and for Derek to change.

The cheerleaders came out first. Some of them acknowledged Sophie, but the entire pack of girls ignored me, which was the norm. Cheerleaders and Nerd Nation were like caviar and bottled farts. They might both smell terrible, but the caviar people thought they were so much better. That's why I was afraid that Sammie would go over to the Dark Side. She was a bottled farts girl, through and through. It would crush me if she joined the caviar crowd.

And then Regan came out, an ice pack on her nose, mumbling about Sammie to Veronica Moore. "She shouldn't even be on the team! She doesn't know what she's doing."

I couldn't help myself. "Lookin' good, Regan," I said, smiling.

She didn't even realize I was making fun of her. "In your dreams, dork!"

Sophie looked at me and said, annoyed, "Really?"

"I was kidding," I said. "She looked like an idiot." I shook my head.

The doors burst open and Randy walked out. He walked toward us, all fake smiles to my parents. "Mr. And Mrs. Davenport, so wonderful to see you again. I often tell my mother how much I enjoyed Thanksgiving at your house last year."

My parents knew better than to fall for his nonsense again. They knew everything I had been through with him.

"We're so glad you enjoyed it," my mother said. "Please give your parents our best."

My dad was more enthused, more so about the game. "Great work out there, Randy. That hook and ladder and oh, the flea flicker. And of course, the 44 Blast."

Randy beamed as he walked by. "Thanks," he said to my dad.

As he passed me, Randy leaned in and whispered in my ear, "I'm gonna get you, Davenfart. The moment you least expect it."

"What if I always expect it equally?"

"Your snark won't save you, Davenfart. Even if you see me coming. I'm like the 44 Blast. Gonna run right over you. Kinda like when you and I played basketball, one on one.

Gulp. I forgot about that. Or the concussion caused me to. I can't remember.

ABOUT THE AUTHOR

C.T. Walsh is the author of the Middle School Mayhem Series, set to be a total twelve hilarious adventures of Austin Davenport and his friends.

Besides writing fun, snarky humor and the occasionally-frequent fart joke, C.T. loves spending time with his family, coaching his kids' various sports, and successfully turning seemingly unsandwichable things into spectacular sandwiches, while also claiming that he never eats carbs. He assures you, it's not easy to do. C.T. knows what you're thinking: this guy sounds complex, a little bit mysterious, and maybe even dashingly handsome, if you haven't been to the optometrist in a while. And you might be right.

C.T. finds it weird to write about himself in the third person, so he is going to stop doing that now.

You can learn more about C.T. (oops) at ctwalsh.fun

facebook.com/ctwalshauthor

goodreads.com/ctwalsh

instagram.com/ctwalshauthor

ALSO BY C.T. WALSH